Heart in Custody

Heart in Custody

A Novel

Kay L. McDonald

Kay L. McDonald

iUniverse, Inc.
New York Lincoln Shanghai

Heart in Custody

Copyright © 2007 by Kay L. McDonald

All rights reserved. No part of this book may be used or reproduced by any means, graphic, electronic, or mechanical, including photocopying, recording, taping or by any information storage retrieval system without the written permission of the publisher except in the case of brief quotations embodied in critical articles and reviews.

iUniverse books may be ordered through booksellers or by contacting:

iUniverse
2021 Pine Lake Road, Suite 100
Lincoln, NE 68512
www.iuniverse.com
1-800-Authors (1-800-288-4677)

Because of the dynamic nature of the Internet, any Web addresses or links contained in this book may have changed since publication and may no longer be valid.

This is a work of fiction. All of the characters, names, incidents, organizations, and dialogue in this novel are either the products of the author's imagination or are used fictitiously.

ISBN: 978-0-595-45141-8 (pbk)
ISBN: 978-0-595-89453-6 (ebk)

Printed in the United States of America

AUTHOR'S NOTE: This story is set in the time period before 9/11, when people with legally issued licenses, documentation, and certification could carry guns and ammunition on airlines in their checked luggage, following airline specifications for the transportation of guns and ammunition.

This book is dedicated to my cousin Shirley who died October 1, 2007. She was my staunchest supporter, cheerleader, and best friend. I will miss her dearly. Love you Cuz.

CHAPTER I

Claudia knew she was in trouble the moment she crossed the threshold of the Lahaina Gardens Hotel and heard the faint, pulsating sound of a security alarm. She looked above the door and saw a red light flashing in unison with the barely audible alarm. As she lowered her eyes, she caught sight of the black-and-white pen sketches of David Keanu, displayed on the one-way mirrored wall with restored photographs of old Hawaiian scenes. David Keanu! The rush of memories caused a slight faltering in her step before the alarm reminded her to stride on. She moved forward and saw a man come out a door to the right, around the corner of the mirrored lobby wall. He motioned to her, and she heard him call, "Miss? Miss!"

She ignored him and looked across the lobby to the dark, polished mahogany reception counter and the twenty-five-foot-wide wall aquarium behind it. A tropical reef of coral provided a backdrop for a myriad of gracefully swaying sea plants and an array of beautiful tropical fish. But they were not what she was looking for. She was looking for the hotel manager, Henri, and he was not there. Nor was he in his office to the right of the aquarium.

A man suddenly stepped in front of Claudia, stopping her in mid-stride. She stepped back, ready to flee. It was a defensive reaction she had acquired the hard way. Not long after her last visit to Maui, she had been grabbed from behind, dragged into the alley, raped and robbed outside her New York office.

With a reassuring smile, the man said in a quiet but authoritative voice, "I need to see you in my office, please."

Claudia stood poised and erect, her eyebrows arched over large gold-flecked, hazel eyes. "You'll have to give me more specifics before I go anywhere with you."

The smile lifted one corner of his nicely shaped mouth apologetically. Claudia noticed the smile did not reach his sea blue eyes, which were intently scanning her. His cleanly sculpted face was tanned and topped with curling, sun-streaked hair that was more blond than brown.

At any other time she would have found him attractive, but not now, when she was still remembering David. Automatically, she categorized him as one of the young, unattached men who lived on the islands for the weather and the water sports they loved. With few exceptions they were handsome, athletic men with muscular bodies who were the envy of mankind. Eying this handsome specimen, she was sorry she hadn't designed a line of clothing for men. It was something to think about for next year.

"I'm sorry for the inconvenience. I promise it won't take long."

With cool reserve, she answered, "I don't understand. Would you please tell me who you are and why I should go to your office?"

He lifted the gold nameplate almost hidden against the bright tropical print of his shirt. "I'm with hotel security, and you set off the alarm when you passed through the door. It won't take but a minute to locate what set it off. It could be your credit cards or keys."

Claudia read the name on the gold badge pinned to his shirt. It did indeed identify him as Chris Hadley of security. "How long has this been going on?"

"Since January, when one of our guests went on a holiday shooting spree."

"Where is the manager?"

"The manager is out of the hotel right now. If you'll just come into my office, we can settle this as quickly as possible."

Claudia stood still, resisting. She wondered how to get out of this situation without causing a scene. She was already aware of the curious looks from people passing through the lobby and from diners seated at the tables in the garden restaurant area to the right of the lobby. The tension she had lost on arrival was returning, and there was no escaping the single-minded man standing before her.

Less demanding, he said, "Look, neither one of us wants to make a scene. We can talk in my office with more privacy, and I can page the manager for you."

There was a softening in his eyes as well as in his voice. Claudia, knowing she really had no other choice but to comply, sighed, "All right."

Chris Hadley smiled and nodded as he stood aside and directed her with an inconspicuous gesture toward his office. She passed him and noticed a very subtle scent that captured the fragrance of the island breezes flowing off the ocean, combining the essence of flowers, sea, and sun. She found the very subtlety of it as provocative as the glimpse of blond curls on his chest.

She entered the small office and was surprised to see evidence of real office work in progress. A phone and papers from an opened file covered the desk. More files were stacked on one corner. On a table behind the desk, a computer hummed quietly, its screen a continuously hypnotic turquoise ocean breaking on a golden sand beach. A two-drawer file cabinet stood in the corner. She surmised that he was employed by the hotel in some capacity other than security. Her estimation of the man went up a notch. Claudia moved to one side to stand in front of the desk. Hadley lowered himself into the chair behind the desk and poked a button on the phone near his right hand. The same hand gestured to the chairs behind Claudia. "Please sit down, Miss ... uh, I'm afraid I don't know your name."

"Jordan. I'd rather stand, thank you." She wasn't going to make this easy for him.

"Miss Jordan. As you wish. Just tell me what you are carrying and we can get this over quickly."

She dropped her shoulder slightly, and the golden chain of her small purse slithered down her arm. She offered him the purse. "You said it could be my credit cards or keys. They're in here if you want to see them." When he didn't take the purse, she laid it on the desk.

He opened a desk drawer, brought out a round, black instrument, and passed it slowly over her purse. It made no sound. "I think I'm looking for something larger than what you can carry in this purse."

"What do you mean?" She looked at him with annoyance.

"There isn't enough metal in your purse to make the wand react like the alarm system did. Do you want to put it on the desk, or do you want me to wand you?"

"This is ridiculous. I refuse to submit to any more of this until I can see Henri."

He stood up and looked at her intently. The blue eyes had turned to steel. His mouth became straight and hard, and his demeanor changed from polite to all business. "This isn't a request, Miss Jordan. I need to know if you are carrying a gun."

She leaned forward, picked up the purse, opened it, and drew out a slender wallet. She opened it to the row of cards and pulled two from a plastic window, offering them to him. One was a driver's license and one a permit to carry a concealed weapon.

"I'm afraid this permit isn't legal in Hawaii, Miss Jordan. May I see the gun?"

She reached inside her tunic-length jacket. From a cleverly designed pocket artfully concealed under the loose tank top, she withdrew a tiny, two-shot derringer and held it out to him butt first.

Hadley took the gun and checked to see if it was loaded. It was. He emptied the two bullets into his hand and told her, "I'll have to keep this in my safe until you leave."

"I have a legal permit to carry a weapon, and you will be violating my rights if you don't give it back to me."

Hadley sighed silently and shook his head, explaining, "I'm sorry, Miss Jordan. It is not legal for anyone to carry a concealed weapon in the state of Hawaii. You will have to leave it with me."

"Absolutely not! You will be violating my right to protect myself."

"Is there someone threatening you?"

"I don't know. Will you be a threat to me now that I have given you my only protection?"

A faint smile softened Hadley's mouth. "Point taken, Miss Jordan. Do you have proof you were trained by a qualified instructor in a police-sanctioned program for the handling of weapons?"

She pulled another card from her billfold and handed it to him. He studied it more carefully than he needed to. The signature alone told him the instructor was qualified, but he took time to compare the picture IDs on the permit, certification card, and driver's license to the irritated woman standing in front of him. Her full name was Claudia Jane Jordan. She was five feet nine, and the pictures hardly did her justice. The permit, license, and certification were all issued in the state of New York.

The door behind Claudia opened before Hadley could ask the question that begged to be asked but was none of his business. Henri, the hotel manager, bustled in.

Claudia turned, smiling with relief at the dapper Frenchman in his white suit, maroon silk shirt, and lei of white orchids.

"Henri!"

Henri's arms opened expansively, and he exclaimed, "Claudia! I am so sorry I wasn't here to greet you, *mon cher*." He hugged her quickly and released her to remove the lei from his shoulders. He placed it over her head, giving her a quick kiss on each cheek before he asked Hadley, "And why is Miss Jordan in here?"

"She set off the alarm with this." He held up the tiny pistol with his finger in the trigger guard. "I was just telling Miss Jordan we would have to keep it in the safe for her until her departure."

Henri looked stricken. "Claudia, *mon cher*, I am so sorry for this inconvenience, but I am afraid it is the law. If there was anything I could do …" He shrugged apologetically.

Claudia sighed with resignation. "It's all right, Henri. I don't blame you." She flicked Hadley an accusing glance.

Henri continued, directing his words to his security officer. "I can vouch for Mademoiselle Jordan. She is one of our most honored guests, and we must make her stay here as pleasant as possible."

It was Hadley's turn to be annoyed, but he smiled and said graciously, "Forgive me for detaining you, Miss Jordan. It's been a pleasure meeting you." He held out his hand as if daring her to accept his apology.

She smiled, but the smile was as cold as the temperature on Haleakala at sunrise. Without offering to take his hand, she said, "You were just doing your job."

As she walked out of the office on Henri's arm, Hadley looked after her with a frown.

CHAPTER II

Claudia opened the door to her suite on the fourth floor, kicked off her shoes, and went straight to the French doors. She opened them wide to the veranda and the ocean breeze blowing in from the island of Lanai across the sparkling blue water. She leaned on the railing of the shadowed veranda and breathed deeply of the sun-drenched air, losing the tension that had returned during her encounter with hotel security. She thought of all the things she needed to do to prepare for the Monday morning opening of her designer clothing show and sighed. She loved her profession, but right now she wanted to be a normal tourist in the islands, have a tall, cool drink, and just enjoy the warm, soft, fragrant breeze.

She headed for the refrigerator and the carton of her favorite tropical fruit juice the hotel had placed there at her request. She filled a glass with ice and poured the juice over it. She returned to the veranda to sip her juice and enjoy being on Maui again. She tried to convince herself she liked being here because the sun was shining. It was gloriously warm, and she hated the cold winter weather of New York. The other reason, which wouldn't be ignored, was David Keanu. He was the real reason she was here. It was David who had changed her life.

◆ ◆ ◆

Claudia's first trip to Maui had been as a model hired for a swimsuit photo shoot at Kaanapali Beach. She was awaiting her camera call in a colorfully bonneted double lounge chair on the beach in front of the Sheraton Maui Hotel. To keep from being burned, she was covered from head to toe in a broad-brimmed hat, sunglasses, and a long white cotton beach cover-up.

A few yards away from her, a man caught her attention. He was setting up an easel, and when he began to paint, she couldn't take her eyes off him. He was a big man, more than six feet tall, with the heavily muscled build of an athlete. He wore only a pair of cut-off jeans, revealing a skin so deeply tanned he had to be Hawaiian. It was a contradiction that fascinated her. He was an artist with the physique of a bodybuilder, and the connoisseur in her took time to peruse him more slowly. She enjoyed the leisurely investigation from the top of his head, covered with thick, curling, blue black hair, trimmed short over his ears but shoulder-length in back, to the ripple of muscles down his broad back. She drew her breath in involuntarily as her eyes discovered, just above the waist of his cutoffs, the discolored ridge of a scar. It was less of a shock when she found another scar on one of his muscular legs. She felt curiosity and sympathy all at once, wondering what had happened to disfigure his otherwise picture-perfect body.

Claudia couldn't contain her curiosity. She put aside the book she had been reading and approached the man, whose face she had not yet seen. He was painting the black, volcanic point of rock jutting into the ocean as it must have looked when only native Hawaiians lived on Maui.

She asked, "Is there something significant about the rock you're painting?"

Without looking at her, he answered in beautiful, flowing Hawaiian.

"I'm sorry," she said. "I didn't understand."

His eyes still on his painting, he answered caustically, "That's right. You haoles have never understood—not then, and not now."

She was surprised at his hostility. After a moment, she said, "I'm sorry if you got up on the wrong side of the easel this morning. I hope you don't need to sell your work for a living because *you* have a lousy attitude."

At the moment she finished her statement, the shoot coordinator approached, waving his clipboard at her. Giving her an impatient look, he announced, "CJ, you're next on camera."

The full, sensual mouth of the man at the easel curved into a smile, as if the comment had caught him off guard, and he turned his head to look at her, but she retreated to her beach chair. As she took off her hat, sunglasses, and cover-up, she noticed him watching her.

Claudia took her position in front of the camera. She was a natural—elegant and long-legged with long, beautiful waving hair the color of rich honey, and unblemished golden skin. Her look was both regal and provocative, her movements graceful and seductive as she followed the cameraman's directions, every pose a picture of perfection.

Three hours later, Claudia was finished. She walked back to her lounge chair to put on her hat and cover-up. The shoot was done for the day, and the rest of the day was hers. She hadn't given the artist a second thought after her earlier inquiry. But when she turned to leave, she glanced his way. Their eyes met, and she couldn't help but look at him. Above the expanse of broad shoulders and beautifully defined chest was a sensuously handsome face. The large, dark, expressive eyes, shadowed by thick black lashes and topped with thicker eyebrows, arched questioningly at her, but it was his mouth that captivated her with the subtle sensuality of his smile. She shivered involuntarily, thinking about being kissed and caressed by those sensitive lips.

"Would you like to see the painting?"

Claudia didn't hesitate. She smiled her acceptance as she walked toward him, tying the hat ribbons under her chin as she went. When she could take her eyes off the artist and look at the painting, she gasped, "That's me!"

"Yes. Do you like it?"

She stared at the painting in awe. There was no mistaking he had used her as the model for the woman in the picture. However, the beautiful image in the painting was from another time, in this place, but centuries ago. The woman was standing on top of a man-made platform of volcanic rock on the crest of the black lava outcropping, sunlight making her hair shimmer like molten gold. Her hips were wrapped in a short tapa sarong. It barely covered one hip and revealed the curve of the other hip, where it was tied below her waist, baring her navel. The only covering on her golden breasts were tendrils of her hair. A crown of vermillion hibiscus circled her head. Her arms were open and beckoning, her hands poised in graceful supplication. But even more stunning was the passionate light in her eyes and the sensual curve of her mouth. Though she didn't see in herself what he saw, she was aware that the camera captured her latent sensuality in every layout she did. It was one of the reasons she was a rising star in the business. But now this man had revealed it even more completely, and her senses reeled from the impact of it.

"It's beautiful! Would you sell it to me?"

His smile was amiable. "We could talk about it over dinner."

She pulled her eyes from the painting to focus on him, momentarily speechless. Then she laughed. "That's the greatest pick-up ploy I've seen yet! How many women do you paint in a day?"

The smile dimmed, and his eyes grew dark. "You're the first one, haole woman," he said with a tinge of contempt.

He turned his back on her and began putting his paints and brushes away. She realized he didn't need clever ruses to pick up women. There were several bikini-clad hopefuls looking his way. Two of them stood just a few feet away, pretending to admire his painting. He ignored them.

Claudia apologized. "I'm sorry. I really am interested in buying the painting. If you can wait a few minutes, I can go to my hotel room and write you a check for it."

He answered without looking at her. "It isn't finished yet."

Disappointment edged her voice. "How long will it take? This is our last day here. Could you have it done by dinner tonight?"

He finished putting his equipment away and turned his dark eyes on her, studying her intently. It made Claudia uncomfortable. She felt unexpected warmth that was not generated by the sun flow outward from the passionate core he had uncovered in her, and it alarmed her.

At last, he said, "I think I can get it done by seven. Where should I meet you?"

"I'm staying at the Sheraton. I'll wait for you in the lobby. Do you have a card?"

He reached a large, long-fingered hand into the front pocket of his cutoffs, pulled out a limp, dog-eared card, and held it out to her. "I'm David Keanu."

She took the card and felt the dampness of it. The thought of where the card had absorbed the moisture—in the pocket next to his groin—made the heat she was feeling rush to her skin in a blush. Flustered, she said, "I'm Claudia Jordan." Then, feeling overpowered by the nearness of him, she turned and walked away.

Claudia dressed very conservatively for her dinner meeting with David Keanu. She wore a sleeveless, ivory, knee-length tunic top, with a mandarin collar, over matching pants and high-heeled sandals—something she could rarely do with most men she dated. David Keanu was tall enough that her five-foot-nine height in three-inch heels would not tower over him. She looked cool and elegant as she waited for him in the hotel lobby. She felt anything but cool, wondering if he would actually come and if she could maintain her poise if he did.

He was late, but when she saw him, all irritation melted. A tingle of excitement coursed through her as he came into the lobby carrying the covered painting. In a muted tropical print shirt, beige pants, and leather sandals, he looked even more handsome than he had on the beach. He moved lightly and gracefully for a big man, in spite of his obvious limp.

She rose to meet him and smiled her delight. "I'm glad you were able finish it."

"No problem." His eyes swept her from head to foot and back again. "Lead the way, haole woman."

She noticed the gleam in his eyes. The subtle inflection of his voice made his words more a term of affection than disdain. She hoped he wouldn't see the flush rising up her neck to her cheeks as she led the way to the Black Rock Terrace Restaurant. To make matters worse, four of the other models working on the shoot were seated at a table nearby, and they gave her knowing looks and coy waves. The hostess seated Claudia and David. Claudia was thankful David was silent while they studied their menus and Claudia regained her composure.

They ordered, and he asked, "Would you like to see it?"

"Of course."

He lifted the painting and uncovered it for her. With all the detail he had added in the finishing process, it was even more stunning. It took her breath away, and she just sat looking at it in awe.

The waitress brought their water and broke the enchantment when she noticed the painting and commented, "What a beautiful painting. Where did you find it?"

Claudia answered, "This is the artist, David Keanu."

The waitress looked at the painting, then at Claudia, exclaiming, "Why, you're the girl in the painting!" She paused then as she made the connection between Claudia and the other four models she was waiting on. "Oh! You're one of the models, aren't you?"

"Yes, I'm CJ."

"Well, I'm impressed. It's a pleasure to meet you." She gave them both a smile before she bustled off.

David asked, "I'm curious. When you introduced yourself to me you called yourself Claudia, yet you told her you were CJ."

"CJ is how I'm known professionally."

"What's wrong with Claudia?"

"There is another very well known model by the name of Claudia. Since I'm a relative newcomer in the business, I had to use a different professional name."

Claudia's fellow models chose that moment to cluster around the table, their eyes devouring David and the painting in the chair between them. She had no choice but to introduce David, who was obviously enjoying the attention his work was causing.

"Mr. Keanu, I'd like you to meet my friends Stephanie, Dana, Georgia, and DeDe. This is David Keanu. He was painting on the beach today."

Stephanie exclaimed, "That's you, CJ!"

DeDe, admiring the artist as much as his work, gushed, "Oh, CJ, it's so beautiful! Are you going to buy it?"

"I was hoping to, but with all this attention it may be priced beyond my budget by now."

Dana teased, "Don't forget you have a curfew tonight."

Claudia's skin grew warm again. "Don't worry."

Georgia, seeing Claudia's growing discomfort, said, "Come on, girls. Let's give Claudia a chance to make a deal."

Too late, Georgia realized the double entendre, and she blushed along with Claudia while David chuckled and the other three models giggled. Georgia, her face as red as her hair, blurted, "I didn't say that! Come on, before CJ starts throwing steak knives at us."

Laughing, they said their goodnights, and Claudia and David were alone again. Claudia remained embarrassed. She picked up her water glass, drinking slowly as she tried to regain her composure.

David, still smiling, asked, "What's this about a curfew?"

Claudia set the water glass down, glad to change the subject. "We fly to the big island in the morning to do more shooting. Rules are to get to bed early so that we aren't carrying more bags under our eyes than in our hands. So maybe we should get down to business. How much do you want for the painting, Mr. Keanu?"

He looked at her intently, compellingly. "I'm easy to deal with. I'll let you have it for fifteen hundred dollars if I can see you again, a thousand dollars if you want to come to my studio after dinner, or free—if you spend the night with me."

The waitress brought their order, but neither one of them touched the food. David Keanu's eyes never left Claudia's, and she knew he could read her reaction. It was difficult to hide her astonishment.

"You must be kidding!"

"Those are my terms."

He gazed at her with intense eyes. She was still reeling from his proposal. Her voice calmer than she felt, she said, "I'll give you two thousand for it—no strings attached."

He stood up. "I don't deal, haole woman." He picked up the painting, covered it, and glanced at her again. "You know where to find me if you change your mind." He walked away.

Claudia watched him leave in disbelief. He was the most infuriating, arrogant man she had ever met, not to mention he'd left her with two uneaten dinners to pay for.

It wasn't until she was tossing and turning sleeplessly in bed thinking about the painting, David Keanu, and the way he had affected her that she realized it wasn't about the money. It was the woman in the painting he wanted.

◆ ◆ ◆

Claudia hadn't noticed the sun set behind Lanai, but the darkening sky finally penetrated her preoccupation, and she banished the memory of David Keanu from her mind, focusing on the task ahead of her. Reluctantly, she went into the bedroom and opened her suitcases. She unpacked and changed into a pair of lightweight cotton pants in a soft shade of moss green and put on the matching loose, sleeveless tunic top painted with bright tropical flowers. It was one of her original designs. She slipped into a pair of low-heeled sandals and left the room. She took the elevator to the first floor, where the meeting rooms and offices of the hotel opened on a wide veranda that circled the open-air courtyard in the center of the hotel building. A tropical garden of palm trees, flowers, plants, and a stream of water flowing over volcanic rocks offered a secluded dining area near the lobby. Beyond the restaurant was the Little Grass Shack Lounge with a deeply shaded palm frond roof and ceiling fans with two bars. One bar faced the dining area, and the second bar overlooked the swimming pool.

She unlocked the door to the mini conference room and flicked on the lights. Her trunks of clothing were lined up like beached whales around the room, waiting for their contents to be hung up. The display panels and racks lay unassembled in cartons on the floor. By Monday morning, she had to be ready for a busy week of selling her island-styled designer clothes.

Claudia had started modeling while in college to help pay her school expenses. After graduation, she spent several intense years working her way up as a high-fashion model before she met David. It was her desire to be with David that had motivated Claudia to pursue her long-range goal to design clothes. Her fashion sense and unique designs eventually won her a place in a well-known house, where her career had flourished along with her love for David.

Claudia quickly made a name for herself with designs for cruise and resort wear. But her love of the Hawaiian Islands, inspired by her love for David, motivated her to slant her designs more and more to clothes designed exclusively for Hawaiian Island wear.

Bringing her designs to the islands had been as much stimulated by her desire to increase her exposure in Hawaii as it had been the incentive to spend more time with David. The plan had worked. Sales doubled the first year and tripled the second year. And this year, she had planned on extending her business trip in the islands with something more significant, even though the affair with David had ended the year before.

Claudia's idea was to offer a free modeling class to girls of high-school age and put on a fashion show for the public as a grand finale. It was her way of doing something for the people and place she had grown to love.

She opened the display rack cartons first. The racks were easily assembled by fitting them together like giant Tinker Toys. Once she had them all assembled, she fastened fabric panels on the front of the racks. Aware of the broad range of heritage of the people who populated the islands, each of her groupings had colors that would complement the varying complexions, from very light to very dark. A sampling of each of her designs and the varying color tones would be pinned to the fabric panels to display them.

It was close to nine o'clock before she realized she was hungry. She hoped the restaurant was still open and left the room, locking the door. She ordered a sandwich to go from the waitress and was walking back toward the elevator when she saw Chris Hadley from hotel security approaching her. She averted her eyes and would have passed by without acknowledging him, except he stopped, waiting for her.

"Hello again, Miss Jordan." His smile was tentative, his eyes questioning.

She nodded but did not reply.

He fell into step beside her. "Hey, I really am sorry about what happened today. No one told me you were coming and that you were not to be questioned even if you were carrying a bazooka."

She faced him with a frosty look. "Okay. If you want me to forgive you for doing your job, fine, but don't think that gives you reason to think we are friends." She turned on her heel and walked to the elevator, where she hit the button with her thumb and stood stiffly with her back to him.

When the elevator doors opened, she stepped in, and he followed her.

"What are you doing?"

"I'm seeing you safely to your room."

This time the smile did light his eyes. They crinkled at the corners and his teeth flashed white in his tanned face. He was quite handsome when he smiled.

"I'm perfectly able to find my room by myself." Irritation edged her voice.

Hadley's grin grew broader, "Oh, but you're a VIP, and you heard Henri instruct me to do everything in my power to make your stay pleasant."

"Yes, I did. And I will be telling Henri tomorrow to inform you I do not require your special attention to make my stay pleasant."

The elevator doors opened, and she bolted between them. Hadley followed her to the door of her suite. Her hand shook as she tried to insert the magnetic card in the door slot. She felt his breath on her neck as he stopped behind her and reached his arm around her, placing his hand on hers. Claudia froze, not knowing whether to fight, or flee. Hadley guided the card into the lock with his hand closed around hers. When the green light flashed, he dropped his hand to the handle and opened the door.

Just as quickly, he stepped away from her and asked, "Would you like me to inspect your room to make sure it's safe?"

She turned sparking eyes on him. "No, thank you. Good night!"

Claudia stepped inside her room and pushed the door closed in Hadley's face, irritated by his amused grin. She leaned against the door and felt the unreasonable anger seep out of her. Tomorrow she most certainly would ask Henri to tell Chris Hadley to leave her alone.

Claudia worked all weekend, setting up and arranging her displays. She didn't see Chris Hadley the rest of the weekend and wondered if he had weekends off. She forgot her annoyance with him and didn't keep her threat to speak to Henri. He hadn't done anything really wrong. It was her problem, and she would have to deal with it.

Monday morning, she was downstairs early to open her display room for her first appointment at nine o'clock. As she opened the door, she saw Hadley coming toward her along the veranda from the employee parking entrance. She wondered if he was just coming on duty. She pretended not to see him and hoped he would pass by her.

"Hello," he said as he stopped behind her, his voice tinged with amusement. "Need any help unlocking doors today?"

Thinking she may have been wrong not to speak to Henri, she answered, "No, thank you." The door swung wide open in her eagerness to get away from the annoying Hadley, allowing him to view her work.

Before she could grab the door and close it in his face, he walked through the opening and gazed around the room at the displayed clothing. "Hey, this is nice. Did you do all this?"

She saw the incredulous look in his eyes and wondered if she could trust his reaction, or if it was only a way of catching her off guard. "Yes. This is what I do for a living."

"You mean selling these?"

Impatiently, she answered, "Not just sell them. I design them, make them, and market them."

"Does that mean you sew them yourself?" His eyes teased her.

Sighing in frustration, she answered, "No. But I do choose the materials for them and have them made to my specifications."

Wordlessly, he walked around the room, looking at each display. He finally said, as he came back to her with a serious look on his face, "I'm impressed, Miss Jordan."

"Thank you. Now if you don't mind, I have a nine o'clock appointment."

"And I have to get on the job. If you need anything, just call me."

"Thank you."

He flashed a lopsided smile at her, "I think you mean that." He turned and walked out of the room.

CHAPTER III

Claudia's last morning appointment was over a little before noon. She went to the hotel restaurant for lunch and was lucky enough to get the last table. She was just finishing her lunch when Hadley appeared beside her table.

"There isn't another table available. Would you mind if I joined you?"

She did mind, but since she was done with her lunch, she offered, "I'm finished. You're welcome to take the table."

His smiled faded as she abruptly stood and left him standing there. She felt guilty about treating him, or anyone, so ungraciously. However, short of telling him in no uncertain terms she wanted him to leave her alone, she didn't know what else to do. If she told Henri to tell him to leave her alone, it could cost him his job. He didn't deserve to lose his job, but she didn't know how else to make him realize she wasn't available.

Her last appointment of the day didn't leave until well after six o'clock and left the door open. Claudia got up to close the door. It was distracting to have people gawking in while she was trying to work. She felt drained, but she also felt good. The lines had sold very well. Halfway to the door, a familiar figure filled the doorway.

"Hi there. Are you done for the day?"

"Not quite."

"I'm off. Would you have dinner with me?"

"Thanks, but no. I have a lot of paper work to do."

His smile dimmed a little, but he answered congenially enough, "Okay. Maybe next time?"

Without changing expression—she didn't want to encourage him—she was about to answer no, then instead, feeling guilty for the way she had been treating him, she answered, "Maybe."

His smile brightened. He said, "I'll consider that a rain check," and left. Claudia wondered what had possessed her. She shut the door and leaned against it. She shouldn't have promised him anything. She had just given him permission to keep asking her out. That was the last thing she wanted. Or was it? She shook her head. She had already changed her life for one man. Did she even want to consider doing that again? Would this man be willing to change his life for her? If he didn't, could she continue to do what she did if she lived in the islands? Did she even want to try? She'd have to know a lot more about Chris Hadley before she could answer any of those questions. It was obvious that he was attracted to her. As heartbreaking as it had been to leave David, she still hoped to find love again. She had to open her heart to the possibility of love at some point in time. Why not now?

The rest of the week went very well for Claudia. She worked very hard at what she did without seeming to. She was always composed, patient, and gracious, never high-pressure. By the end of Saturday evening she was exhausted, but feeling extremely pleased with how sales had gone. She wanted to celebrate, but there was no one to celebrate with. Involuntarily, an image of David crossed her mind and made her heart wrench with an ache she thought she had long since gotten over. She should have known better. Her love for David came back to haunt her every time she even thought of these islands.

It was after nine o'clock. Even the hotel dining rooms would be closed now, except for the lounge. She didn't feel comfortable going into the lounge by herself. She started picking up the papers, still scattered on her desk from the last buyer, and stapling them together. There was a soft knocking on the door. She looked up as the door opened.

Chris Hadley stuck his head through the narrow opening and said, "Hi! You're working late. Have you eaten?"

"No."

He stepped into the room and smiled at her. "Then I'm here to collect the rain check you gave me."

He wore a cobalt blue shirt with random swirls of white orchids. It brought out the blue of his eyes and accentuated his tan. She noticed he wasn't wearing shorts, but a pair of tan cotton slacks. He was a very attractive man, and he had been nothing less than a gentleman every time they met. The hard shell of her resistance softened as she thought of spending another evening alone. She deserved a little celebration, and she couldn't celebrate her success without company. She smiled back at him, "All right. Where do you suggest?"

"The Hard Rock Café is only a couple blocks away."

"Good. I could use the walk and some fresh air."

He opened the door for her, his grin dazzling in his tanned face. She walked past him into the hall and smelled the subtle fragrance he wore again. It reminded her she had been hours without freshening up. She asked, "Do I have time to visit the ladies room?"

"Of course."

A little bit of cool water on a towel applied to her cheeks, forehead, neck, and arms helped revive her. Fresh lipstick, a dab of cologne, and running a comb through her hair made her feel more presentable. Chris was leaning against the veranda railing surrounding the garden area when she came out of the ladies room. She was conscious that her Oriental-style, knee-length dress of champagne silk fit her slender body like a glove. He straightened up and offered her his arm. They walked through the quiet lobby, down the steps to Front Street, and turned south, toward the downtown area of Lahaina.

The Hard Rock Café was noisy and packed with people. They waited on the sidewalk for a table. The huge windows facing Front Street were open, and the noise from inside made it difficult to hear. Chris stood so close to her she could smell the aftershave he wore and feel the warmth of his breath on her face when he spoke.

He asked, "Have you eaten here before?"

"Yes." She didn't elaborate.

He commented, "You look like you're done in. Maybe we should go someplace where we won't have to wait and it's quieter."

"No. I'm okay. It has just been a long day." After a long pause, she asked, "Why were you working so late tonight?"

"I usually work from nine to nine for the hotel, but once in a while my relief man will come in early during the week and, if there's no crisis, I can leave."

"That makes a long day for you, doesn't it?"

He grinned at her, and she could see a teasing sparkle in his eyes. "Yeah. I don't get too many gun molls setting off the hotel security system."

"Seriously, how often do you have to stop someone?"

"More often than you'd think, but most of the time it is something other than a gun. Usually it's a man who has a pound of keys in his pocket, or a Swiss Army knife. Once in a while we get a gun, but not often."

"What happened to make Henri think a security system was necessary?"

"Some guy with a grudge against the world came in during the Christmas to New Years week without reservations and demanded a room. The hotel was full, but he didn't believe the desk clerk and pulled a gun on her. She fainted, and the rest of the desk clerks started screaming. The guy fired his gun into the tropical fish tank behind the desk and released a few hundred gallons of water, plus fish, all over the teakwood floor before he ran out of the hotel."

Claudia laughed. "Oh, no! Poor Henri. I bet he was purple."

Chris grinned. "Yeah, and he knows some pretty purple language, too."

She looked at him inquiringly. "Were you there?"

"No. But I heard all about it when he hired me. His memory hadn't dimmed any."

Just then, they were called for a table. They followed the host through the crowd of people around the bar on the lower level, where a 1959 Cadillac convertible hung suspended above the bar. It was reputed to belong to Elvis Presley. The rest of décor carried out the pop music theme, with pictures, records, and musical instruments belonging to various artists.

They stepped up to the upper level, where there was a table for four available near the back railing separating the tables from another bar. She took the chair closest to the railing, and Chris went around the table and took the other chair near the railing. The host handed them menus. Claudia was famished and directed all her attention to the menu.

Claudia noticed that Chris glanced only briefly at the selections, found one, and closed his menu. She could feel his eyes on her. It never failed to happen when Claudia wore this dress. The keyhole opening from the neckband of Claudia's dress grew provocatively wider as it plunged to the cleft between the firm golden fullness of her breasts.

The server came with water-filled glasses and took their order. Chris had to almost shout for Claudia to hear him across the table. "What will you do now that you're done with the marketing part of your trip? Will you be going back right away, or taking some vacation time?"

"I plan on staying for a while." She was hesitant to tell him her plans, but he would find out anyway. "Monday I start interviewing girls for my style show."

"Really. Are you looking for models?"

"Not professionals. I have placed an ad in the paper asking for teenage girls who want to learn about modeling."

"Why do that when there are trained models for hire?"

"I want to work with the younger girls—especially girls who may not have the opportunity to go on to higher education. Learning the disciplines of modeling will help them have confidence to overcome their backgrounds, whether racial, cultural, or environmental. If I can help just one girl think she can do something with her life, other than work at a minimum-wage job, I will feel I have contributed something useful to all of them."

"That's a pretty lofty goal and a great idea. I like it."

Their food came, and Claudia attacked it hungrily, as she did everything from her work, her ideals, even life itself. She felt Chris's eyes on her and looked up. He was looking at her with more than just casual interest. He was looking at her with what she could only describe as something deeper, something more profound that touched her heart. She blinked and dropped her eyes. She had thought she was ready to fall in love again, but now she wasn't so sure. It was too soon, and why Hawaii? She closed her mind to all thoughts except her food.

In the middle of their dinner, there was a commotion at the entrance to the café. Claudia looked up, her face turning pale as she heard a voice she recognized. A party of three men and three young, attractive women were crowding through the front door. Claudia's heart stopped as she saw David. She ducked her head, hoping he wouldn't see her. The last thing she wanted was a scene, but in spite of her determination to forget, the memories came flooding back, as real as if meeting David had happened only yesterday instead of several years ago.

◆ ◆ ◆

After David had left her sitting in the restaurant at the Sheraton Hotel with two uneaten dinners, Claudia should have forgotten him, but she couldn't. In spite of herself, she was attracted to him. For Claudia, that meant learning everything she could about his culture. She wanted to understand the man. Before the photo shoot was finished on the big island, she had bought a dozen books on the history and culture of Hawaii.

Now, months later, she was finally returning to Maui to do a shoot for a resort and cruise catalog. She now understood the significance of Black Rock to the Hawaiian people. Before the missionaries began to influence the Hawaiian culture, Black Rock had been an ancient temple site, or *heiau*, a place of worship for the ancient Hawaiians. In David's painting, she was standing on top of the *heiau*. There was also a legend attached to Black Rock. Kahekili, a powerful chief who ruled Maui and the near islands of Lanai, Molokai, and Kahoolawe, proved his fearlessness by jumping into the ocean off the point of Black Rock, where it was believed human souls crossed into the land of the dead.

Claudia arrived on Maui on Saturday. Sunday, she took a cab into Lahaina from the hotel at Kaanapali, where the crew was staying and some of the shoot would be done. Front Street in Lahaina was clogged with people and traffic. The cab turned onto a narrow side street and stopped in front of an old, two-story, wooden building. David's art hung in the front windows.

"This is it, lady."

Claudia paid the cabbie and stepped out of the cab. She entered through the open door. David was talking to a couple. His back was to her, but his voice, soft, deep, and rich, raised gooseflesh on her arms. She wore the outfit she had worn the night she had last seen him, plus a wide-brimmed straw hat and sunglasses. She looked like any tourist just off the cruise ship anchored off shore—the cruise ship they would be using in their shoot on Monday.

She immediately saw the painting of her hanging on the wall. It hadn't lost its impact on her. It was even more stunning than she remembered, since she now knew she was looking at a sacred temple used for worship and sacrifice. It brought another surge of gooseflesh to her arms. Was she a goddess, or the sacrifice? She pulled her eyes away from it and concentrated on David's other paintings. They linked a Hawaii that no longer existed with a contemporary one. He was painting the history of his ancestors, and she saw his native soul in every one. He was as good as the best artists she had seen displayed in the galleries in Lahaina.

Finally, the couple left with their purchase, and David approached her.

"Aloha. May I help you with something?"

Without looking at him, she asked, "How much is the painting of the woman on the *heiau*?"

"That painting isn't for sale."

She turned to face him. "Are you going back on our deal?" She removed the dark glasses, seeing first amazement and then amusement in his eyes. Then a smile barely turned up the corners of his full, sensuous mouth.

"What makes haole woman think we've still got a deal?"

"You told me to get back to you when I made up my mind. I'm getting back to you."

"Which is it? A real date, or do you want to spend the night with me?"

"Correct me if I'm wrong, Mr. Keanu, but you said nothing about a real date. Your exact words were, 'if I would see you again.' I am seeing you again."

He laughed, and she would have enjoyed the throaty sensuality of it if he hadn't been laughing at her. She felt a blush of embarrassment rising toward her cheeks. Not wanting him to see how he affected her, she turned and walked out the door.

He caught up with her on the corner of Front Street.

"Hey, wait a minute, haole woman."

She stopped and waited for him. She didn't resist as he took her arm and steered her into the shade of an awning.

"Did you have something more to say to me, Mr. Keanu?"

"It's David, and I have a lot to say to you."

"It's CJ. Are you ready to make a deal that isn't a proposition?"

He grinned at her, and the effect was like melting butter in a microwave. "I'm willing to discuss it. My friend, Cowboy Kapana, is opening his new bar in Makawao and celebrating his first national recording contract. I would like a real date. I'm asking you to join me."

"When you say 'real date,' just what does that mean?"

He chuckled and shook his head, and Claudia knew he was still laughing at her. "It means I'm taking my mother and my bruddah's little sister to help with the luau, which leaves me without a date to call my own. You are what I would call a real date."

It didn't take her long to consider it. Having David's mother and a friend's sister along made it seem less threatening. "All right, but we have to agree on something—I need to be back at my hotel before ten o'clock."

He laughed, shaking his head. "Either you come with no strings attached, or we'll forget it right here."

Claudia didn't want to forget it. For too long, she had focused on being a success instead of on relationships. She was attracted to this man and wanted to see where the attraction would go. Her job slate was clean. She'd never violated a curfew or caused a problem before. The worst that could happen was that she would be released from this job and sent packing. Was it worth the risk? If David Keanu hadn't been standing right there waiting for her answer, she might have decided it wasn't worth getting a blemish on her otherwise spotless reputation. But he was standing there, his presence was overpowering, and she wanted that painting.

"Okay. What time do you want to pick me up?"

He laughed. "Okay, haole woman. I can pick you up at five o'clock. Where are you staying?"

"The Hyatt Regency, Kaanapali."

His smile swept away any doubts that were left about going out with him, except for what to wear. "Is this a formal affair?"

"Only as formal as you want to be. I don't get any more formal than jeans and an aloha shirt. I'll see you at five."

She caught a cab back to the hotel, feeling excited and giddy as a schoolgirl on her first big date. She had never felt that way about anyone before. No one had ever affected her like David Keanu. No one had ever been as physically attractive to her, or as honest with her as he was. She knew where he was leading her, and right now, she wanted to follow him.

◆ ◆ ◆

A shadow passed through Claudia's eyes and she dropped her head toward her unfinished dinner. She wanted to hide. Her hand raised to her cheek protectively. She saw Chris look beyond her to see who was coming in just before she dropped her eyes to her unfinished dinner.

Chris asked, "Do you know those people?"

She gave a brief nod. Claudia saw a shadow pass over Chris's face. Did he know David, too? If he did, would he also know that she had been involved with David? There had been a big splash in the local newspapers from the opening of Cowboy Kapana's Bar in Makawao, complete with a headline about local artist David Keanu involved with a New York Model known as CJ. Chris had looked at her clothing displays. Had he noticed that her clothes had the label CJ of New York?

As luck would have it, the large table in the center of the raised area just beyond them was being vacated. Keanu and his party barged through the exiting people toward them. The host at the entrance looked chagrined, but he clearly didn't want to confront the belligerent group and cause more of a scene.

Claudia shifted in her chair, trying to hide herself as David approached, hoping he wouldn't notice her. He stopped as he reached her table, and Claudia held her breath, hoping he would go by.

"CJ? Is that you?"

Slowly, she turned her face up to him. It was like being hit in the stomach by a New York cab on Fifth Avenue. He was so devastatingly handsome: dark, curling hair, milk chocolate skin, smoldering, black velvet eyes, and she loved him still. The breath rushed out of her, and she felt faint.

She could barely speak his name. "David."

His hands framed her face, lifting it up as he bent over her. Then his full, sensuous mouth covered hers. When he took his lips from hers, he smiled knowingly. She was still his, and he knew it. "When did you get in? You should've called me."

"I didn't have time," she stammered.

"Baby, when did that ever stop you?" He kissed her again.

A woman's voice protested. "David! Are you coming? I'm hungry."

He straightened up then, and Claudia breathed again. It was then David noticed the man sitting at the table with her.

"What are you doing with *him*?" David's eyes narrowed with animosity. "He is not someone you should be seeing, baby. Come to my table. I don't want you with him. Not now. Not ever."

David giving her orders was the last straw for Claudia. In a low voice, she warned, "You have no right to tell me who I can see and who I can be with. Now, please, David, just leave me alone."

Keanu took hold of her chair and pulled it back with a jerk. Claudia was almost unseated and cried, "David!"

Chris got to his feet and said in an even, authoritative voice, "The lady told you to leave her alone, Keanu. I suggest you do as she asks."

David grabbed Claudia's wrist and pulled her to her feet. "Come on, baby. You're coming with me."

Claudia struggled to free her hand. "No!"

Chris was coming around the table as a waiter was closing in on the scene. The waiter grabbed Keanu by the shoulders. It was a mistake. Besides being taller than anyone else in the room, David was heavier, reflecting the Hawaiian side of his heritage. He was also a very strong man from his years of hard physical training for the Iron Man Triathlon—a combination, when mixed with alcohol, that was volatile. He dropped Claudia's wrist, and she scrambled between the chair and table, trying to get away.

David Keanu hurled his strong, two-hundred-fifty-pound body backward into the man who had laid his hands on his shoulders. They went crashing into the table behind them. Claudia watched in horror as the heavy, round, wooden table, supported by a single pedestal, tipped over. The three startled diners added their voices to the melee as their food, dishes, and glasses went crashing to the floor.

David struggled to his feet just as two more of the staff joined the fray. He stood his ground, ready to fight both of them as diners scrambled to get out of the way. A Hard Rock Café bouncer was coming from behind David, along the railing on the bar side. He was carrying a billy club.

Claudia cried, "Look out, David!"

He heard her, turned in time to see the blow coming, and tried to step out of the way. He stepped into a puddle of food and drink on the floor and slipped, losing his balance. He grabbed for the table. It rolled under his weight. He stepped backward to keep from falling, his right foot thrusting through the railing behind him. He struggled to stay upright and free his foot. One waiter tried to wrench the table away from him as another waiter tried to grab him. David ducked, trying to twist away, releasing the table with one hand as he took a swing at the waiter nearest him. His left foot lost traction in the mess on the floor, and David grabbed for the table again. The waiter rolled the table away from him and he went down heavily, his caught leg twisted between the rails. The bone snapped. With an anguished cry of pain, he fell facedown amid the broken glass, cutting his face.

Claudia, the fear for herself changing to fear for David, scrambled to his side. Blood from the cut on his face was already turning the water on the floor red. She turned to the suddenly stunned group and shouted to be heard over the loud rock music, "Someone call nine one one!"

Chris was on the floor beside her, handing her his handkerchief, and Claudia pressed it to the bleeding cut. David was dazed and moaning. She heard the young woman's voice she had heard before and looked up. She recognized her now. It was Rosa, the sister of David's lifelong friend they had taken to the Cowboy Kapana opening. Only now she was beautifully grown up and crying hysterically. "He's going to bleed to death! Do something! Please, do something!"

In a few moments they heard a siren outside, and the police came storming through the front door of the café. Chris rose to talk to them while Claudia searched for ice cubes on the floor to hold on David's face.

They soon heard another siren, and medics came pushing through the crowd gathered at the side door of the building.

"Okay, lady. Can you give us a rundown?"

They started working on David before she answered. "Broken ankle, I think. This cut on his face is bad."

"We got him, lady."

She felt a hand on her shoulder and looked up. Chris offered her his hand. She took it, and he helped her to her feet. The police were ushering the rest of David's party out the door. One remaining policeman bent to handcuff David.

"We're going to transport him, lady. You know him? You can come along and give us his information."

Without hesitation, Claudia answered, "Of course."

Chris said, "I'll come with you."

Claudia shook her head. "No. It'll start all over again if you're there. I'll be all right."

Chris looked at her, seeming to weigh the circumstances. He nodded and said, "You know where to find me if you need me."

She returned the nod and followed the stretcher and the policeman out the side door to the ambulance, passing the encased electric piano on the wall emblazoned with the name, "The Beatles."

CHAPTER IV

Claudia spent the rest of the night with David at the emergency care center in Lahaina. David had been arrested for being drunk and disorderly. There would be a fine and a court appearance, and a judgment from the Hard Rock Café for damages. David was still out cold. He had stitches holding together the cut on his face and a cast on his broken ankle. It would be a while before he would cause any more trouble. Claudia had arranged bail for him so he could recuperate at home instead of in jail.

She was by his bedside when he awoke in the morning. She was feeling a little worse for wear herself. He opened his eyes slowly, put his hands to his head, felt the bandages, and moaned, "Where am I?"

Claudia answered, "In the emergency care center. How do you feel?"

"Like a sugarcane truck ran over me." Then he focused on her and realized it was Claudia. "CJ! What happened, babe?"

"Do you want the official police report?"

"No. Just tell me how bad it is."

"The short version is, you broke your ankle and have nine stitches in your face."

He grinned, but the grin soon became a frown, as if it caused pain. He reached for her hand, and she let him take it. "At least you stuck by me. I knew you didn't mean it when you said we were through."

"Wrong, David. We are through. If I wasn't sure before last night, I am now."

"Oh, come on, baby, you still care for me. You wouldn't be here if you didn't. It'll be okay. Just wait and see."

"No, David. It won't be okay. I'm not sticking around to pick up the pieces. I'll do what I can to help you, but it's not going to be like it used to be."

The doctor came in just then and said, "He can be released now. Do you have someone to take you home, Mr. Keanu?"

David looked at Claudia. She nodded her head. "I have a car. I can take him home."

"Good. I'll have someone fit him for crutches and get a wheelchair. Where is your car?"

"It's at the hotel. I can get it and be back in a few minutes."

"We'll have him ready when you get here."

Claudia left the room thinking she would walk to the hotel. It was then she realized she was still wearing the blood-spattered dress she had worn to dinner. She decided to call a taxi instead of walking. She had the taxi driver take her to her car in the hotel parking garage. She would get David home first.

David's living quarters were in the loft above his studio. She pulled around behind the building, where there was barely room to park one vehicle, let alone two. But David's vehicle was a Jeep CJ5, and she had a small sports car.

She helped him through the backdoor into his studio and looked balefully at the flight of stairs going up to his living quarters. "I don't think you can manage those. Can you?"

"Who cares? I've got you with me, and that's all that matters now. C'mere, baby."

His crutches clattered to the floor as he pulled her into his arms, his mouth devouring hers. She pushed against him at first, fighting his ardor, but that didn't last long. He had a magic about him. He was intense, passionate, and he knew how to make her surrender. She forgot all the reasons she had left him and returned his kisses, wanting him, needing him, remembering all that had been good between them and remembering the night of their first kiss.

◆ ◆ ◆

It had all began six years ago as Claudia waited for David in the lobby of the Hyatt Regency Hotel. He was on time, and she smiled her pleasure at seeing him as she stood up to meet him, noticing, too, that his limp seemed worse. She looked at his feet. He was wearing cowboy boots. Did the boots make his limp more pronounced? She raised her eyes and forgot the limp when she viewed the snug-fitting jeans accentuating his muscular thighs. His T-shirt, advertising Cowboy Kapana's Bar, was almost hidden under the fragrant beauty of two plumeria and orchid leis. He was a striking man in any crowd. More eyes than just hers found him attractive, but his eyes admired only her.

Claudia wore a white, halter-neck dress that bared her golden shoulders and back and plunged between her breasts to an empire waist. The dress was gored to flow over her slender, feminine hips, and it flared to fluted ruffles at the hem just below her knees.

David smiled and said, "You are a picture beautiful enough to paint, haole woman." He lifted one of the leis from his neck and lowered it over her head, lifting her hair with care and letting his hands rest momentarily on her shoulders with gentle pressure from his fingers for emphasis. His touch was warm and promising.

"This is lovely, David, and it smells so beautiful. Thank you. And you already have."

"What?"

"Painted me. Remember?"

He grinned and said, "You won't let me forget. Are you ready?" He offered her his arm, and she took it, letting herself barely touch him with her fingers, feeling them tremble as she rested them on his warm skin. Heads turned as they went down the stairway toward his bright red Jeep parked in front of the hotel.

The highway into and out of Lahaina was busy. The parks along the highway were full of families enjoying weekend picnics and water sports in the gently lapping water along the narrow, sandy beaches.

"How far away is Makawao?"

"About forty miles."

"And you said this party was for a cowboy? Somehow, when I think of Hawaii, I don't think of cowboys."

David chuckled. "Well, think again, haole woman. The up-country on the flanks of Haleakala is ranch land, and for years, Makawao has held a rodeo every Fourth of July. One of the oldest and largest ranches is on the big island. The Parker Ranch shipped beef to California during the gold rush. Three of the Parker Ranch cowboys, or *paniolos*—that's Hawaiian for cowboy—competed in rodeos on the mainland and took championship honors back in the early nineteen hundreds. The Ulupalakua Ranch on the southwest slope of Haleakala has a statue of Ikua Purdy. Ikua was a descendent of Jack Purdy, who worked with John Parker and was one of the first Hawaiian cowboys."

"That's a great story, David. But I didn't see any cowboys in your paintings."

"You're right. It's a part of our history I need to work on."

"And who is this cowboy who is having the party tonight?"

"Cowboy Kapana? He is a cowboy, but he is also a musician, singer, and dancer. His music caught the attention of somebody in the recording business, and he is going to the mainland to make his first album."

David slowed the Jeep and shifted as they turned off the main highway and started the gentle climb upward through fields of pineapple and sugarcane toward Makawao. In Hawaiian, "Makawao" meant "where the forest begins." The forest here being giant eucalyptus, ironwood, and jacaranda trees bordering rich, green pastureland ideal for cattle. At a crossroads with highways leading to the roads to Hana and Haleakala, Makawao had its own persona, mixing the old west with new age.

The main street of old buildings, looking like a western movie set, sloped upward, clinging to the slope haphazardly. The street was lined with cars and a few horses tied to hitching posts. David wheeled the Jeep into what appeared to be the last available parking space.

"We'll have to walk from here. Cowboy's got a crowd."

Claudia heard the music before they reached the rusting, metal-sided, two-story building-turned-tavern. The voice she heard was singing in Hawaiian, and it was beautiful. As they entered the crowded tavern, the singer began a song in English. The tavern was full, and every table was taken. The air in the room was heavy—the ceiling fans were unable to cope with the crowd and humidity—but the room was hushed, held quiet by the performer on the stage. Several musicians backed up the singer. They were dressed informally. The singer was dressed only in a sarong; his rich, coffee-colored skin glistened with perspiration. His long, waving, black hair was loose, and held off his face with a headband of shining green leaves. He was a wiry man with a broad chest and bowed legs.

There were cheers and applause as he finished his song. He used a towel draped over a tall drum to wipe his face. Then, poised behind the drum, he began to chant in his native tongue, emphasizing his words with the drum. Claudia marveled at the range the man had. All the songs and chants were in different tones. As the last chant ended, the rest of the musicians raised their instruments. The drummer began. Cowboy Kapana sprang from behind his drum and, with a series of leaps and poses, he became a warrior dancer from an ancient time.

Claudia was fascinated. Her skin prickled with the intensity and emotion the performer exuded. The other musicians softly picked up a countering thread of music, and the warrior on the stage turned his back to the crowded room. As the guitars and ukulele music hushed the drums, the dancer began to sway, his arms and hands flowing with his hips and flexing feet as he slowly turned back to his audience in a sensuous, beautifully expressive hula.

The crowd rose to its feet at the end of the performance, shouting and clapping. Claudia joined them enthusiastically.

"What do you think of him?" David shouted in her ear.

"He's wonderful."

The performer hushed the audience and said, "Mahalo. Thank you. You're the greatest. Let's take a break and bring on the luau!"

He jumped off the stage and came through the crowd of people, stopping to shake hands and receive his well-deserved accolades. The stage behind him was suddenly swarming with people as long tables were set up and women came from the kitchen area adjacent to the bar with platters of food.

When the performer reached the back of the room, he recognized David and came to where they stood.

"Brah! I thought you don' make it!"

Their hands clasped warmly. "I wan bring this wahine for you show. She over Lahaina way. She CJ."

Claudia looked between the two men curiously. They had lapsed into a pidginized dialect she had not heard David use before. Likewise, the talented singer's vocalizations had been precise.

"Hey, CJ." He held out his hand to Claudia.

She smiled and took his hand. "I loved your music and dancing."

David said, "Cowboy is not his real name, but nobody can pronounce it, so we call him Cowboy."

A moist, warm, brown hand held on to hers as Cowboy said, "Very glad meet you. Where David find you?"

David answered, "I found her under a rock. Black Rock."

Cowboy's eyes widened with recognition, and he suddenly lost the pidgin speech. "You're the woman in David's picture! Wow! You're even more beautiful than the picture. It's a real pleasure to meet you, Miss Jordan."

"The pleasure is all mine. I'm surprised it took someone so long to find you. You have so much talent."

Cowboy's faced flushed with embarrassment. "You sure know what to say. Whatever you want—it's yours!"

Claudia grew serious. "Well," she smiled, "I'd love to be able to learn the hula the way you danced it."

"Deal, wahine. Right after the luau, I'll give you your first lesson—on stage." He grinned rakishly.

Claudia blushed, stammering, "I didn't really mean—"

Cowboy raised his hand and interrupted. "No problem. I done my whole gig. You're going be to be the rest of the show, lady."

He grinned, pulled on Claudia's hand, and motioned her to follow. "Come on. You can join me at my table."

Claudia gave David a stricken look.

David laughed and waved her forward. "You're committed now, CJ."

They followed Cowboy to his reserved table at the front of the room. He led them onto the stage and turned to his audience. "Enjoy this luau my family and friends make for you, and don't go away. I got a treat when you finish. The show's not over!"

Claudia, already flushed with embarrassment, followed Cowboy Kapana to the head of the food line. An overwhelming amount of island food was spread before her. She took small portions of each dish, not knowing what some of it was. She hoped she could discreetly ask David what she had on her plate once they were at the table.

Claudia set her plate on the table and gave David a dismayed look. "What am I eating?"

David named the obvious. "You have kalua pig, *lomilomi* salmon, sweet potatoes, and long rice. This purple stuff is poi. You'll have to ask the cooks what the rest of it is."

Claudia, starving, wasted no more time with questions and proceeded with the food adventure. Most of it was tasty, but she decided poi had to be an acquired taste of starving people.

David was done eating, and he asked Cowboy, "One of the boys got a joint, brah?"

"Sure. Squid got one."

Claudia choked, "Squid?"

Cowboy laughed and explained, "Yeah, he play like he got ten arms." He scooted his chair back and went to find his musicians.

David leaned over, pointed to the round medallions on her plate, and said, "I forgot to tell you. This is squid."

Claudia looked at what she thought was fish and grimaced. "Now you tell me."

David laughed. "Did you like it?"

Cowboy was back. He held out his hand to David. "Squid want to know if you'll be training for the triathlon this year."

David took several hand-rolled joints. He stuck one in his mouth to light it before he shook his head and said, "I don't think so. Not this year, anyway." He dragged deep on the joint, adding, "Thanks, brah. I owe you one."

"No problem. You hurt?"

David nodded as he inhaled again.

Claudia tried to mask her disapproval, picking up on Cowboy's words and remembering how much worse David's limp had seemed when he had come into the hotel. Her curiosity was escalating. She watched David closely and saw him begin to relax. The marijuana was taking effect.

When everyone was finished eating and the tables were cleared away, Cowboy took Claudia's hand. She followed him as he led her toward the stage. They stopped at another table, where the ladies who had served the luau were sitting. He touched a teenage girl on the shoulder. "You come, too, Rosa. You can help."

Delighted, Rosa followed Cowboy and Claudia onto the stage. Cowboy waved the crowd into silence and announced, "We have a special guest. She is a friend of bruddah David Keanu. She is big-time model from New York here on a job and wants to learn how to hula." He smiled ruefully. "Please welcome Claudia 'CJ' Jordan and brah Puna Halupa's sister, Rosa."

The crowd clapped encouragingly. The musicians started playing softly, and Cowboy faced his guest dancers. He looked at Claudia's feet and whispered, "Lose da shoes, wahine."

Claudia kicked off her shoes and felt a flush rise to her face as the audience laughed.

Cowboy ignored them and instructed in perfect English, "Relax and start with the hands. Just move them with mine. Listen to the music. Feel the rhythm. Sway with it."

Claudia blocked everything from her mind except what she was doing. The ability to focus on what she needed or wanted to do had helped her through many stressful moments and given her the inner strength to achieve her goals.

An hour later, Claudia was exhausted but exhilarated. Though Cowboy's quick sense of humor had often left her helplessly laughing, her innate grace and ability to learn quickly overcame her initial awkwardness. Cowboy applauded his pupils and turned to the audience. "Give these two wahines a round, folks. They've been good sports."

Claudia was glad to leave the stage and collapse in her chair as the audience rewarded their efforts. Rosa was giggling, her dark eyes glowing.

"That was so much fun!"

David's eyes were shining with approval at Claudia, but he included them both in his praise. "You were great."

Cowboy followed them off the stage and, putting his hand on Rosa's shoulder, said, "Hey, brah, bring these two wahines to my studio when I get back. They got potential."

He leaped back on the stage, motioned to the musicians, and broke into song. For another hour, Cowboy Kapana enraptured his audience before he sang his closing song.

It was then that David led Claudia to the kitchen area, where his mother was finishing the luau cleanup.

"Hey, Mama. Are you ready to go home?"

One of the women turned around at the sound of David's voice. There was no doubt in Claudia's mind who she was. The resemblance between her and David was telling. She was tall and stately, carrying her weight well. Her black hair, shot with silver strands, was pulled back and held in a wreath of white hibiscus.

"Mama, this is Claudia Jordan. Claudia, this is my mother, Malama Keanu."

A beautiful smile lit the older woman's face as she embraced Claudia. "Aloha, Claudia. David's picture doesn't do you justice. But you did look like you have our blood in you on the stage tonight."

Claudia blushed and answered, "Thank you. It's so nice to meet you."

"Where's Rosa?" David asked.

Malama answered, "She's here."

Just then, Rosa appeared with a cloth-covered basket. "Do we really have to go?"

David put his arm around the girl and grinned. "Yes, my little hula wahine."

As soon as they were outside, David lit another joint, and Claudia noticed his uneven gait all the way to the Jeep. David opened the driver's side door for Rosa, and then helped his mother into the backseat from the opposite side. When he returned the seat to its upright position and turned to Claudia, she asked, "Would you like me to drive?"

David's eyebrows arched at the question. "Why? You think I can't?"

"I don't know. You tell me."

He placed his warm hands on her shoulders and gazed intently into her eyes. "Look at me, haole woman. It takes a lot of this stuff to bring me down. Ask Mama and Rosa if they think I can drive."

Rosa responded, "He's okay, CJ. I never see him stoned."

Malama added, "It's the only thing that kills his pain and helps him drive." She paused, and then admonished David, "You shouldn't be wearing those boots."

David laughed and Claudia acquiesced. "Okay, but will you promise to let me drive if I ask you to?"

"That okay with you, Mama? Rosa?"

Both women answered in the affirmative. David helped Claudia into the Jeep, limped around to the driver's side, and they were underway. He wheeled the Jeep up the hill and through the town of Makawao. Claudia read the signpost at the intersection. They turned onto Highway 365 to Hana.

The drive through the eucalyptus-forested hills was cool and fragrant. Rosa bombarded Claudia with questions about modeling, and Claudia answered the girl as honestly as she could. When they reached the Hana Highway and began the twisting traverse between lava cliffs and sweeping moonlit views of the ocean, Claudia marveled at the vistas around every corner until she began to feel queasy. Claudia asked, "Does anyone have any water?"

David looked at Claudia, and then in the rearview mirror. His mother and Rosa were leaning against each other, sound asleep. "What's wrong? You sick?"

"Yes. I forgot to mention I get seasick on winding roads and boats."

"There's water up ahead at the park. Can you make it that long?"

"I'll try."

It was all Claudia could do to make it around the next corner, let alone the several miles to the park. When David pulled into Kaumahina Wayside, she opened the door and barely made it out of the Jeep before she threw up. She retrieved her purse and dug for her Dramamine as David was waking up his mother and Rosa.

"Wake up, Momma, Rosa. We're taking a little break here." He struggled out of his seat and came around the Jeep to Claudia. "The water fountain's over here." He took her arm and led her to the water.

Claudia swallowed the pill and drank from the fountain to wash it down. Wiping water from her chin, she said, "I'd better use the restroom while I'm here."

"You going to be okay?"

"In a few minutes, I hope."

When everyone was settled into the Jeep, they were underway again. Not many miles farther, David turned off the main road onto a dark, narrow road leading downhill. They passed a church and then some houses. David pulled into the yard of one of the structures. It was built several feet off the ground. Dogs came out from underneath the house, crying in hound voices at their arrival. A light came on in the house, and a shadowy figure filled the door and yelled at the dogs to be quiet.

David stepped down from the Jeep and helped Rosa out. David called, "Hey, brah. I got your little sis here."

"Hey, bruddah. Where you been all night?"

"We went to Cowboy's party. You missed it, brah."

"Yeah. Went up da mountain huntin' today."

"Have good luck?"

"Yeah. I got some for you."

David glanced at Claudia. "I'll be right back."

In a few minutes, David came out of the house. The stocky man stood on the porch, watching David until they had backed out into the road and started back up the hill.

Claudia asked, "That's where Rosa lives?"

"Yeah. That's her brother, Puna. He and I go way back."

"How far back is way back?"

"We went to school together. I was raised on this side of the island back up the road at Keanae village. He was raised here."

"Where's here?"

He chuckled, "Wailua."

David turned on his blinker after they had traveled a couple miles back the way they had come, and they were going downhill again. "This is where I grew up. Mama still lives in the house I grew up in. Over there on the right are the taro patches. Ahead of us, that white building you see is the church. The story is that the church was built from coral our people gathered from the ocean."

David pulled off the road into a yard not far from the church building. The house looked similar to the one where they had just left Rosa, except there were flowers along the front. The headlights shone on a porch with a rocker. David got out and helped his mother out of the Jeep.

Malama said, "It was nice meeting you. I hope we meet again."

Claudia answered, "The pleasure was mine."

David saw his mother inside and returned to the Jeep. In a few minutes, they were back on the road.

"Is your mother your only family?"

"Yes. My grandparents are dead. I never knew my father. He was a fisherman. He and my mother were to be married when he got back from his last trip out. He never came back. Mama figured he died in a storm out there." David nodded toward the ocean, glimmering in the moonlight.

"Did your mother ever marry?"

"No. It might have been easier if she had."

"How do you mean?"

"We were pretty poor. We lived with my grandparents. My grandfather was a fisherman, too. My mother and grandmother worked very hard in the garden and taro patch to feed us. They sold what we didn't need to support us."

"Your father must have been a handsome man."

"Oh? Why do you think so?"

"His son is. Was he full-blooded Hawaiian?"

"No. My mother is. My father was Portuguese. I use my mother's family name, Keanu."

They gained the highway and rounded a corner, and the faint lights of the village at Keanae were out of sight.

"Does she still have to work as hard to make a living?"

His teeth flashed in a grin. "Well, no, she doesn't. I have asked her a dozen times to come live with me, but she won't. She says Lahaina is too busy and too noisy. She has a job that's easier now. She's housekeeper for the church. She gets enough pay to get by on, and I do what I can to help her, but she is a proud woman. She gets her back up when I try to help her beyond what she thinks is being a good son."

"She sounds like a wonderful woman. I'm sorry I didn't talk to her more, but I was afraid she didn't approve of me."

"She's just shy. She doesn't know you. She thinks I should marry Hawaiian. She believes in the old ways, and she inspires me to keep those old ways alive in my work."

Claudia fell silent and just gazed into the night, smelling the heavy, moist fragrance of the wind that whipped her hair. She saw flashes of waterfalls when they crossed the narrow, one-way bridges over stream gorges. The headlights showed her glimpses of glistening black cliffs, where ferns and orchids clung at the edge of the narrow winding road. Most of all, she felt the undeniable magnetism of the man next to her.

At last, they reached the improved road. David reached into his pocket, pulled out a joint, and lit it, drawing in deep before he let the smoke out. He took the joint from his mouth and held it out to Claudia. "Want a smoke?"

There was an edge to her refusal. "No, thank you. I don't smoke."

"Why? Have you ever tried it?"

"No, and I really don't want to. And frankly, I don't approve of anyone who does."

"I hear a lot of hostility in your voice, CJ. There are some legitimate uses for this stuff. There are people in so much pain that their only relief is marijuana."

She saw his scars and his limp in her mind's eye. "I apologize for the blanket condemnation, but I still don't think that makes it excusable. There are legitimate pain medications available."

"I have them. But I can only take so many of them in a day. On a normal day, I can get by with just the legitimate pills, but today has not been a normal day. I hoped you would understand this is the only way I can control my pain."

"I'm sorry, David. I want to understand, but it's hard for me to believe there isn't something the doctors can do for you. What does your physician say? Have you gone through therapy?"

"Yes, I had therapy, but my therapist said there's not much more that can be done. I have nerve damage."

"I saw the scars on your back and leg. What happened?"

"I had a bad accident about two years ago. I had ridden my bicycle to the top of Haleakala and was on my way back down. I still don't know who or what hit me. I woke up three days later in the hospital. I had a concussion, a broken back, and a badly damaged leg. The surgeons performed miracles. Otherwise, I wouldn't even be on my feet. But there was nerve damage in my leg and back. That is where the pain is. They couldn't fix that. Everyday living aggravates the condition, and it steadily grows worse. Without the help of this stuff, I don't know that I could handle it."

"Cowboy said something about training for the triathlon tonight. Was that what you were doing?"

"Yes. Do you know about the triathlon?"

"Some. We used to watch it on television when I was a kid. What was it—you had to swim so far, bike so far, and run so far? I wondered then how anyone could possibly do all that and survive to the end of the race. It sounded more like torture than a sport."

He laughed. "You're nearly right. You have to swim two and four-tenths miles, and then bicycle one hundred twelve miles. You finish with a run of twenty-six and two-tenths miles."

"And you did this? No wonder you have the body you do. And you said you never won?"

"No. I guess I'm too big. I could outswim them and came pretty close to outbiking them, but the wiry little guys could outrun me."

"Do they hold it here?"

"No. It's held on the big island now, but it began on Oahu in 1978. Early in the seventies, some guys were arguing over which one of the three sports took the most endurance. They decided to find out, and the Ironman Triathlon was born."

Claudia asked no more questions. She truly felt sorry for David's situation, but to continue seeing him would mean she would have to accept his use of marijuana. It was a compromise she didn't want to make. Surely there was some way help him.

"There's a good place to go for a midnight swim before we reach Lahaina. How about it?"

"I don't think so. It's so late. I'd better not."

"It's too late to worry about it now. Right?"

"Will it make the painting any cheaper?"

He laughed. "That depends."

"On what? I *have* practically spent the night with you."

"My idea of spending the night with me didn't mean in a Jeep."

"Did it include a swim in the ocean?"

"I'm improvising at this point. Unless you want to come to my studio and sleep in my bed?"

It was Claudia's turn to laugh. "I don't think so—on all options."

"Okay, haole woman. I will take you to your hotel."

The traffic through Lahaina was minimal, and in a few minutes they were in the turn lane to Kaanapali. When they approached the Hyatt Regency, Claudia said, "You can just drop me off at the front lobby."

"No way. You are my date, and I see my dates to their door."

"David, really, there's no need for you to do that. My room is in the far building, and I know you are hurting."

"That's what I smoked the joint for."

He parked the Jeep, and she waited for him to come help her out. In spite of the conflict in her, she liked David and liked how she felt with him. There was something in him that she was drawn to, and when she looked up into his soft, deep, dark velvet eyes, she saw an answering warmth as he gazed at her, his full, perfectly shaped lips smiling softly in response. She wanted to feel those lips on hers.

She took his arm and walked silently beside him, relishing the strength and vibrant warmth he exuded.

"This is a beautiful hotel. You must be coming up in the world."

"Not really. They want to use this setting for part of the shoot. We got a good deal because of the advertising benefits the hotel will reap from the catalog."

"Ahhh."

They walked through the shops with their beautiful displays and finally into the hallway leading to the rooms. They took the elevator to the upper floor.

"If you're on the ocean side, I bet you have some view."

"It's fabulous. But then, I just love being here. It's warm, the sun shines, and it doesn't snow or sleet. I could stay here the rest of my life."

"That's what all the haoles say."

She stopped at her door and turned to face him. "This is my room. Thank you, David, for inviting me. I really had a wonderful time."

"You're not going to invite me in?"

She laughed softly. "I think that would be dangerous."

"Even if I promise not to stay?"

"Somehow, I'm not convinced that you will not make me regret letting you in."

He gave her a devastating smile. "Try me and see."

She was feeling his intensity and flushing with the response her body had to him. She turned to the door and ran her card through the lock. The light flashed, and she stepped inside, flipping on the light switch. She moved to the French doors, opened them, and stepped out onto the veranda. The sound of the ocean and the cooling breeze calmed her racing senses.

David joined her at the rail of the veranda. "This is really nice. And so are you, haole woman."

She turned and started to speak, but her words were smothered by his lips softly caressing hers. His strong arms surrounded her and pulled her close. She closed her eyes and reveled in the sensation of his lips, warm and imploring on hers.

It was a long moment after his lips left hers before she opened her eyes and focused on his face. His thick, black eyebrows were arched in question over his dark, glowing eyes.

She stuttered, "David, I …" But his fingertips fell as softly as feathers against her lips, forbidding speech.

He whispered, "Don't talk, baby. Just feel."

He replaced his fingertips with his lips, and she moved into the kiss, tasting his lips, her hands sliding up his hard, muscled chest to rest splayed against his incendiary warmth. His hands moved up her back, and she felt him unbuttoned the three buttons holding the halter top of her dress. She stepped back, reaching for her dress, but he held the ends in his hands and lowered it before she could stop him. She tried to cover herself with her hands, but he stopped her, holding her hands in his as he gazed at her full, firm breasts.

"Ahhh," he breathed softly, "I'll have to retouch the painting. I didn't do them justice."

"David," she protested, trembling inside.

His hands released hers and slid up her ribs until they cupped both breasts, then gently covered the dark rosettes. Claudia's breath caught in a small gasp as her nipples peaked against the warmth of his palms. The trembling inside radiated throughout her as she felt a strange, aching need sweeping through her. She felt faint, and she swayed into the hands caressing her. He moved closer, his hands gliding over her ribs and bringing her into his arms again. His lips claimed hers, and she opened her lips in surrender.

Claudia laced her fingers through his thick, black hair, tasting him, feeling the heat of his mouth like a torch against hers. She was powerless against the desire that left her weak and wanting.

His breath was hot against her cheek as he whispered, "Easy, baby. Easy." His lips moved, burning a path to her ear. She tried to control the tremors running through her. He kissed her neck and shoulder. His lips moved like velvet heat down to the fullness of her breast, where they gently surrounded her nipple. She quivered as his lips caressed her, arching toward him, wanting more as her breasts ached with their own need to be fulfilled. Then, when the hot, moist tip of his tongue touched the tender, swelling bud at the center of her russet areola, she felt a corresponding burst of moisture released deep within, and ensuing convulsive contractions in the place where she felt the aching need for him. She released her breath in a long, shuddering gasp.

David raised his head to gaze into her wondering eyes and whispered, "Oh, baby, how sensitive you are—and how needy."

Claudia closed her eyes, wanting to steady herself, wanting to hold back the tears that suddenly lurked beneath her lids. She took a deep breath and felt calm returning. She let her hands slide from David's hair and felt him take them in his. She felt his warm, soft lips kiss her damp palms. Her eyes opened and released the tears she had held captive behind her closed eyelids.

David saw them and raised his hand to wipe them away. "Don't cry, baby. The night isn't over. There's still plenty of time to take you there again. And again, if you want to go there with me."

With the calming effects of release overtaking her, reason returned. She knew she was in deep and dangerous water. She closed her eyes against the imploring depths of his and placed her palms against his chest with gentle resistance. "No, David. Not tonight. This is happening much too fast. I need time to think about where this is going. I'm not sure yet that I want to go there."

He smiled at her. "Okay, haole woman. But it felt like you wanted to go there to me."

He released her, and she pulled her dress up and fastened the buttons at her neck. His hand touched her cheek, and his eyes smoldered on hers for a moment before he whispered, "I can wait."

He went inside, pulled off his boots, and stretched out on her bed. Claudia followed him, dismayed. "David! You can't stay here!" But David was already fast asleep.

There was only one thing to do. She went into her bathroom and got ready for bed. She returned to the bedside stand, picked up the phone, and dialed the room next door.

A very sleepy voice answered. "Hello."

"DeDe. It's CJ. May I come sleep with you?"

"CJ? Why?"

"I'll explain. Just come open your door."

"Okay."

In moments, she was inside DeDe's room. DeDe sat on her bed, cross-legged and questioning. "All right, CJ. What is going on?"

"David's in my room."

"Oh, my God! What are you going to do?"

"Nothing. I'm hoping he'll be gone by morning. All I want to do is go to sleep."

◆ ◆ ◆

But Claudia had not been able to go to sleep that night with David's kisses and caresses still stirring her blood. She had been wide awake when DeDe's alarm went off. She had returned to her room and David was gone. She had breathed a sigh of relief, but it was premature. The shoot director met her at the hotel restaurant, motioned her aside, and said, caustically, "I'm disappointed in you, CJ. This is totally unacceptable, and you know it. You were out after curfew, and when I called your room this morning, a man answered the phone. You're dismissed from this assignment. Turn in your hotel key and plane ticket. I'll talk to your agency after I get back to New York."

In spite of being sent home from that assignment, the memories of that first date had brought her back to him. He had found the path to the passion he had painted, and she was driven by the need to explore it. She knew there would be no turning back, but by the time she had come to that decision, she was ready to let him take her where-ever he would lead her. All too clearly, she remembered the journey.

No matter how hard she tried to deny it, the magic was still there. He had just proved that to her and now David was asking, "Come make love to me, CJ. Baby, I've missed you so much," while his tongue traced the outer and inner curve of her ear, ending at the lobe, where his lips gently caressed her.

She yearned for the physical and emotional release she had tried to deny she needed since she had left David. She realized that, like an alcoholic, she could not just take one drink. If she let him seduce her now, she would lose herself again, and she could not allow that to happen. It was a hard choice. No man had ever attracted her like David. No man had ever been able evoke the physical and emotional responses David did. She didn't think another man ever would, or could. She pushed forcefully out of his arms, crying, "No!"

She forgot David had nothing to lean on except her, and he fell heavily to the floor. She reacted with horror and went down on her knees beside him. "Oh, David. I'm so sorry. Are you okay?"

He lay there a moment, pain clouding his eyes, and then reached for her with a rueful smile. "Well, that's one way to get me down on the floor so you can make love to me."

"Will you be serious?"

"I am serious." He started tugging off his shorts.

Claudia stood up and said, "If you don't stop, I'm walking out of here, and you can just lay there until your ankle heals and you can get up."

He pushed himself up to a sitting position and said, "Oh, come on, CJ. You know you want me. Admit it."

"No. Will you behave, or shall I leave?"

"You wouldn't leave me like this, would you? After all we've meant to each other? I can't stay here. I can't get up those stairs. Be reasonable, CJ."

Claudia knew what he was getting at. And she didn't even want to consider it. "What about Rosa? Give me her number, and I'll call her."

"Rosa's going to California. You're the only one I've ever wanted, babe. You said you'd help me. I don't see any other way to do this but to go to your hotel until I get a walking cast."

Claudia couldn't think of a way to get out of it. She finally conceded. "All right, but you are not going to interfere with my work or my life. If you can't agree to that, I'm out of here, and you can just lay there until someone comes looking for you."

"And after all we've meant to each other, too. God! CJ, you drive a hard bargain. Now help me up." Then he added, with a seductive smile, "Please."

Somehow, Claudia got David to his feet. He had a lot of strength in his arms; otherwise, she wouldn't have been able to do it by herself. While David sat on a chair at the foot of the stairs, Claudia packed some clothes for him out of his closet upstairs. She had no trouble finding what he needed. She had stayed overnight with him more than once, sometimes for several days at a time, before she had finally admitted to herself that David was addicted to drugs, and he was never going to change. Not for her; not for anyone.

As she pulled into the hotel driveway, she regretted her decision all over again. In spite of her early resistance to Chris, she found she actually liked him. He would not understand what she was doing with David. The bellboy got a wheelchair and wheeled David up the ramp sloping off the end of the veranda. Claudia carried his bag. She was thankful Henri wasn't in the lobby. She didn't want to explain David to anyone.

With David comfortable on the sofa in her suite, she went to take a shower and change. She had a lot of work to do before Monday. She dressed in an ivory T-shirt she had designed herself. It was open at the sleeves and side seams and appeared airy and cool. Soft lacings of matching fabric held the solid pieces together. The matching shorts gave the illusion of being open to the waist, but the open work weaving gradually became closed as it neared the waist and was backed by a liner so nearly matching her skin tone it was hard to tell skin from fabric. She pulled back her thick hair, which kinked even tighter in the humidity—especially today, when there was hardly any breeze blowing off the water—and confined it with a scrunchie that looked like a ring of vermilion hibiscus.

She came out of the bedroom. David looked up from the TV program he was watching and whistled. "You're one sexy babe, CJ. You're damn lucky I can't get off this sofa, or I'd take you to bed whether you wanted me to or not."

She ignored his remarks and went into the kitchen. She made lunch out of fruit and bagels she kept in the fridge. It wasn't going to be easy to keep focused on her next project with David distracting her. Somehow, she was going to have to keep herself under control, and that included what happened in her room. She was the example of what she was going to attempt to do. At the moment, the thought of turning teenagers into runway quality models was daunting enough without adding David to the equation.

After lunch, she took the stairway down to the main floor to avoid the tourists using the elevator. She unlocked the door to the room, where her racks of clothing stood as she had left them the night before. She went to the louvered walls and opened them wide to let what little air there was into the stuffy room. She turned on the ceiling fans. Right now, in the airless humidity of the room, a swim in the hotel pool sounded heavenly.

She was in the middle of removing the last fabric panel from the racks and folding it away in a trunk when there was a knock on the door. She turned as the door opened and Chris stepped inside.

He closed the door and just stared at her for a moment. He found his voice and said, "Hi, are you okay?"

She nodded. "I'm fine."

"Would you like some help?"

"I'm almost done. Isn't this your day off?"

"Yeah, but Barry called in sick. How'd things go with Keanu?" He came to where she was standing and looked down at her. She knew her subtle makeup had not been able to totally hide the dark circles under her eyes. "Did you get any sleep last night?"

"No. I stayed with David all night. We didn't get out of emergency until this morning."

He frowned at the word "we." He said, "And Keanu?"

"He's in a cast, but he'll be all right."

"Where do you want me to start?"

"What?"

"I said I came to help you. What can I do?"

"Nothing. Really. I'm leaving the rest of these up with the clothes on them. I'm using the clothes in the show."

"Can I take you to lunch?"

"No, thank you. I had something before I came down."

"Okay." He shrugged. "I can take a hint. You know where to find me whenever you do need some help."

"Thank you, Chris. I'm sorry about last night."

He shook his head and smiled. "Don't be. I enjoyed every minute I spent with you."

Without another word, he turned and walked out the door, closing it behind him.

Claudia stared at the door for a long moment, her feelings in turmoil. Chris was a nice guy. She could tell she had just hurt his feelings. She had hoped they could be friends, but she knew that would be just as impossible as she and David being lovers again.

CHAPTER V

David had been in pain the rest of the day. The painkillers the doctors at the emergency care clinic had given him had worn off. She gave him what they had sent home with him, but it wasn't enough to keep him from hurting. He didn't want to eat the supper she cooked for them.

"CJ, you've got to go to my place and bring me some of my stuff."

"You know how I feel about you taking drugs, David."

"What kind of person are you to let me suffer like this? My God, Claudia! I can't take it anymore!"

She knew he was upset with her. He only called her Claudia when he was angry. She also knew his tolerance for pain had decreased as his dependence on drugs had increased. Finally, when she'd had enough of his moaning and pleading, she agreed to go to his studio and get the drugs he demanded. She didn't like it, but he was beside himself. She knew there was a limit to what he could endure before he would become violent.

It was just like the old days: Claudia condoning his addiction to the drugs and the drink. Only now it was worse. He had smoked marijuana before, but now he was on cocaine. He could have been before, but she had never seen him use it. Now she had to help him with the injection. She knew she had been right to give up their relationship. It was a relief for both of them when the cocaine eased his pain and he finally slept.

Claudia stayed in the room with David all day on Sunday. She gave him a sponge bath and cleaned the wound on his face, watching for any sign of infection. She had worried about bathing him, but he was so full of drugs he was incapable of doing anything more than trying to talk her into going to bed with him. It was difficult to have him touch her and not respond to him. Every fiber of her being remembered what a sensitive and sensational lover he was. It would be easy to succumb to him, but she knew she couldn't. She would only destroy herself.

When she finally had David comfortable, she went over the entries she had been getting in the mail from the girls answering her ad for the fashion show. They had to write letters and include pictures—not just school portraits, but full-body pictures. There were dozens to go through. She arranged them in alphabetical order. She read through them at least once and sometimes more, marking the ones she felt were the most promising applicants.

On Monday morning, she started interviewing girls. By Friday, she had chosen two dozen out of nearly one hundred who had come for interviews. Some of the girls were dropouts, and some had skipped school to come to the interview. Some were out of school and working at minimum-wage jobs. Some had no jobs at all and lived with their families.

Because a few of the girls were still in school, she set some of the training sessions for after-school hours. She held other sessions in the mornings and evenings to accommodate those who had day jobs. It made a long day for Claudia, but she had fewer girls to work with at a time, and she could work more closely with each girl.

As was to be expected, some of the girls were very quick to learn. Others had a harder time picking up the moves, poses, and turns that became as much a part of a model's life as her makeup and diet.

She had chosen one girl in particular who seemed to be in need of having someone believe in her. A few of the girls were Caucasian. Most represented the Asian cultures or had mixed bloodlines. But one girl appeared to be a full-blooded Hawaiian. She was a tall, ungainly, and shy girl of sixteen and a high school dropout. She did field labor, working on her family's truck farm on the slopes of Haleakala. She was big-boned and large for her age, reminding Claudia of David. Like David, the girl was solid and strong from hours of intensive labor. She was also very self-conscious and shy because of her size. Though awkward and slower than anyone else in the group, she was more than willing and tried harder than anyone to accomplish the finer points of modeling.

After the day of working with the girls was over, Claudia had to care for David. He did very little for himself. He was incapacitated more from the drugs he was using to kill the pain than the cast on his leg. Her suite smelled of his sweat and the joints he smoked. At least he was cheerful, though it was a drugged kind of cheer.

"Hi, babe. God, I've missed you. What took you so long, anyway?"

"Remember, I told you I would be gone all day. Did you eat the sandwich I left you?"

"What sandwich? I don' remember nothin' about no sandwich."

When he was smoking pot, his language reflected his island roots. She was getting angry. "You also didn't remember I asked you to go outside on the veranda to smoke."

"I can't get there an' you know it."

She put the groceries away and opened the French doors and the louvered wall panels to air out the living area. Then she went into her bedroom to open it up and change into shorts and a tank top.

David had done nothing to even try to move. She came out and stood before him, blocking his view of the TV screen. He looked up at her from the sofa with dilated eyes. "Come into the bathroom. I'm going to give you a bath."

"That sounds good, baby. How're we goin' to do that with this cast?"

"I'll figure out something." She handed him his crutches and helped steady him as he pulled himself up. He went a couple of steps toward the bedroom, lost his balance, and went crashing to the floor.

She was on the floor in an instant, helping him to untangle from the crutches. He looked up at her with a dazed look and said, "I can't."

"Can you crawl?"

"Jus' leave me alone."

"I'm not going to leave you alone. It would help if you'd get off the stuff."

"Don' lecture me, baby. I'll get off when I don' have no mo' pain."

"Well, you can't lay here in the middle of my floor."

"How 'bout if I lay in de middle of your bed?"

"That's even less desirable."

He ran his hand up and down her leg and grinned at her. "But you're very desirable, haole woman. Come down here an' I'll show you."

She pulled away from him and said, "No, David. I'm going to get us something to eat. When you get into the bathroom, I'll come help you get washed up."

"I'm not hungry for anything but you."

She gave him an exasperated look and left him on the floor.

By the end of the second week, she had the hotel set up a runway in the room she was using and had the girls come in on the weekend to practice together. The first time they were all together was a comedy of errors. There were giggles and tears as they got accustomed to each other and learned how to walk on the runway while everyone watched. Claudia coached from every vantage point with a microphone to provide instant feedback about what they were doing. She knew she was being tough, and when they were beginning to get disheartened, she had them all sit down. She sat on the edge of the runway and told them, "Okay girls, just relax and pull yourselves together. You've all been working very hard, and you all have accomplished so much. Don't give up now just because you are making mistakes and I am pointing them out to you in front of everyone. You have to go through this to build the kind of poise it takes to be a model—or to be anything else in this world you want to be. You have to learn to play it cool. You have to learn not to let the world stop you from doing what want to do, whether it's being a model or being a hostess in one of the hotels here in Lahaina.

"Accepting criticism for what it is and learning from it are part of building character. I'm not saying that all criticism should be taken to heart. Someone could be critical for selfish purposes, and you have to know how to tell the difference. You have to be able to understand first of all why a person is criticizing you. Do they want to help you, or do they want to hurt you? Ask yourself this question. Does Claudia want to help me? Or does Claudia want to hurt me and make me feel stupid?

"You all should know by now I want to help you reach your full potential. If I haven't made that clear to you up to this point, I want you to understand it now. I want you to be the best you can be. Only by being the best you can be, are you, and let me emphasize *you*, going to be happy with yourselves. I will do everything to help you reach that goal. If you think I'm criticizing you unfairly, come to me and we'll discuss it." Claudia paused and searched each solemn face before her.

"Most of all, I want you to enjoy what you are doing. If you aren't having fun, then you don't belong here. Are there any questions?"

A hand was raised. It was Mikko, the Japanese girl. She had been the last of the girls Claudia picked because she was really too small to be a model, but she had style, grace, and was a natural beauty. "Yes, Mikko?"

"How do we know where you're coming from? You have probably always been beautiful."

Claudia smiled ruefully. "I'm glad you brought that up. I put together some pictures of me when I was your age and going to high school." Claudia slipped a tape into the VCR she had been using to show the girls actual videos of everything pertaining to modeling, emphasizing the hard work and discipline it took to keep in shape and the hours of time that went into being beautiful.

She pushed the play button on the control and the big-screen TV lit up. Claudia was silent as a picture appeared on the screen. The figure in the picture was wearing glasses with one lens covered in black. The person was smiling, showing buck teeth, and had short and very curly hair. It was hard to tell if they were looking at a boy or a girl. A birthday cake with lit candles hid most of the rest of the figure.

Claudia narrated. "This is me on my sixteenth birthday, the summer before I started the tenth grade. We lived in a small town in the Midwest. My dad worked at a hardware store. Mom stayed home and raised us kids. I was the youngest of three children. I have two brothers, so I grew up being sort of a tomboy. I'm wearing glasses with one lens covered because I had what was called a lazy eye, and they were trying to correct it. As you can see, I also had buck teeth. We didn't have enough money to correct both problems at the same time."

The still pictures she had transferred to video showed her opening packages and then standing up, holding a new dress up to her shoulders. It was the first picture of her showing how tall and gangling she had been. She had no shape at all.

"As you can see in this last picture, all my growth to this point had been up and not out. All through school I had been about the tallest kid in any of my classes, even taller than the boys, and I had a nickname from the first grade on. Anyone want to guess what it was?" No one was willing to guess, so Claudia told them. "I was called 'The Stork.'" There were only a couple of giggles in the room, and Claudia realized the video was doing more to give her credibility than anything she might say.

The next picture was from her high school yearbook. She was in the back row and the tallest girl in the picture of a girls' basketball team. "In our small town, there were no sports programs until we got into high school. Dad put up a basketball hoop for my brothers, and I played with them. I got pretty good at shooting baskets and faking out my brothers, but the high school didn't know that. Because I was tall, I was asked to be on the girls' basketball team. I was shy and self-conscious, and I refused at first, but the coach of the team was a woman who wouldn't take no for an answer. She kept telling me how much she needed me on the team, and I finally agreed to try out. She made me feel like I was important from the first day. She began to work with me, helping me realize I did have something to offer. When I finally said I would play on the team, it was the turning point in my life."

The rest of the video showed film taken at basketball games in which Claudia "The Stork" Jordan turned into a powerhouse basketball player. As the video film rolled, Claudia finished her story. "By the time I was in my senior year, our basketball team was ranked number one in the state. If you will look closely, you will see in the close-ups I was wearing braces on my teeth. My mom went to work after I got into high school to pay for the work I had to have done to straighten my teeth and to help pay for my college."

The last of the basketball scenes showed Claudia holding the state basketball trophy. The next scenes showed her in cap and gown as she graduated from high school with honors and a scholarship. The tape ended, and Claudia turned the VCR off.

"If it hadn't been for a high school basketball coach who believed in me, I wouldn't be where I am today. She didn't give up on me, and I'm not going to give up on you until every one of you can do this the way I know you can if you do your best."

They were all silent and looking at her with new respect and resolution. She smiled at them and said, "All right. Take a break. Go get something to drink and freshen up. Be back here in twenty minutes."

Like schoolgirls at the closing bell, they rushed for the door. Claudia smiled after them. She was tired, but it was a good tired. She sat on the edge of the runway, flexing her shoulders and stretching her tired muscles, trying to relax for the few minutes the girls would be gone.

A male voice asked, "Is school out for the day?"

It was Chris. She smiled and answered, "No. We're just taking a break. What are you doing here today?"

"My weekend to work. How's it going with the girls?"

"Good. They're having a little problem today getting used to working the runway and having everyone watching, but they'll get over it before the weekend is over."

"I saw the big one. She doesn't exactly look like the model type. How's she doing?"

"Not too bad. I think she'll be fine."

"Aren't you giving someone like her false hope that she could ever be a model?"

"No. That's where you're wrong. She can be a model if she wants it bad enough. That's what I'm trying to teach them by doing this. They can do it if they are willing to work hard enough."

He shook his head. "I think you're wrong there. Not that one."

Claudia smiled knowingly. "Just wait and see."

The girls started filing back into the room with their soda pops. With wide eyes and coy smiles, they admired the tan, handsome blond man wearing an aloha shirt and khaki pants. He looked like the centerfold out of a male hunk magazine. Claudia heard the whispers and giggles as they took their seats.

Chris grinned, his skin getting a shade darker, and said, "Well, I'd better get back to work. Good luck."

She nodded and watched him leave. The luck she needed was not with these girls. They would be fine. Where she needed luck was with David. He was doing better. His pain was finally subsiding. He was able to get around on his crutches fairly well now. She would be taking him to the doctor in the middle of next week. She was hoping she would be able to convince him to go back to his own place as soon as he saw the doctor. She had been able to understand his need to kill the pain, but now that his pain was better, he still demanded the drugs. She found herself giving in to his demands because it was the only thing she could do to pacify him until she got him back to his own place.

At five o'clock, she dismissed the girls. They had worked even harder since the break. They were finally coming together as a group and helping each other. The more accomplished girls worked with the girls who weren't quite in sync. She was having fun now, and the tiredness she had felt earlier was gone. And she could spend more time with Nani Li'i, who was having the most trouble.

Finally, she asked, "Nani, can you dance?"

"What you mean by dance?"

"The hula."

"Oh, sure. Been doin' that since I was a baby."

Claudia smiled, an idea beginning to form. "How would you like to hula down the runway?"

She shrugged. "Maybe."

"Let's try. I'll do it with you."

She called the other girls who were practicing on the runway to attention and had them clear the runway. They went to their seats as Claudia and Nani Li'i stood at the head of the runway. Claudia turned her back to everyone, facing the girl, who looked graceless.

"Okay, Nani. Let's hula."

Since the night at Cowboy Kapana's party, she had gone to his studio for hula lessons every time she had come to Maui. It had also been a convenient place to meet Rosa and teach her the basics of modeling. Though Rosa seemed enthusiastic and eager to learn, Claudia did not see in Rosa the spark that she had to have to succeed.

Claudia had gotten quite good at the hula. Now, using her hands, hips, and feet, she slowly moved backward down the runway, encouraging the shy Nani Li'i to follow. The girl, feeling embarrassed with all eyes on her, was stiff and inhibited, but Claudia felt that, with enough work, she could get the girl to be less self-conscious, and the idea she had began to take shape in a new and exciting way.

At five o'clock, she locked up the room after the last girl left. She walked out the front door of the lobby, heading toward the Cannery Mall and the Safeway store to get some things for supper. Returning from shopping, she could smell the distinctive odor of marijuana smoke in the hallway as she neared her door. She opened the door to her suite, furious with David for smoking in the room while he watched TV. A smoky haze greeted her.

She set her groceries down and strode in between David and the TV, blocking his view. Angrily, she ordered, "David, take that outside. You know I don't like you smoking in here." She stormed into the kitchen.

He flicked off the TV, hoisted himself to his feet, got his crutches under his arms, and thumped into the kitchen. He stood there watching her while she put groceries away.

"You know, CJ, you've become a real bitch. Why don't just relax and tell those kids to go to hell? You and I could have some fun if it weren't for those damn kids you think you can turn into models."

"And you are wearing out your welcome with me, David. The day I take you to see the doctor, you won't be coming back here."

He leaned his crutches against the counter, caught her around the waist, and pulled her to him, kissing her neck. "I'm sorry, babe. It's being so damn helpless. I get bored. I can't paint, and you're gone all day with those kids. I don't have anything to do but to sit here and smoke and watch TV. If I didn't have the weed, I'd go nuts. You know that."

She nodded, "Yes, I know that. Now please let me go so I can fix us something to eat."

He leaned against the counter, turned her around, and pulled her against him. "I'm hungry for something all right, but not what you brought from the store."

He kissed her long and well, but the smell of marijuana on his breath and the fact that he still couldn't bathe completely and took little interest in trying helped her resist what he was offering. Another part of her was aching for him and wondering how she was going to be able to resist him until she could get him out of her suite and out of her life.

She pushed against him until he finally released her. Still angry, she said, "You've got to stop this, David. I have no intention of going to bed with you. It's over—really over."

CHAPTER VI

On Sunday, Claudia and the girls started putting the show together. She selected the clothes they were to wear and started organizing them into groups according to her lines of clothing. She determined how they would follow one another down the runway. She brought in a CD of Hawaiian music to play when she and Nani Li'i practiced on the runway while the other girls took a break outside the room. If she could get Nani to loosen up when no one was observing her, she felt she had a chance to make her dance in front of everyone. She turned on the CD player and started to dance backwards down the runway, coaching the self-conscious girl.

Claudia had taken her sandals off, and her long, narrow feet moved in time to the slow, sensuous swing of her hips. The long, slender fingers of her hands flowed in graceful, sweeping movements, telling the story of the music playing on the CD. The music was "The Hawaiian Wedding Song."

Nani, who had been trying to imitate Claudia's movements, suddenly stopped dancing.

"What's wrong, Nani?"

"It's that guy. He was watching us."

Claudia turned her head toward the door. There was no one there. "What guy?"

"That cute, blond guy. I think he's security, or something."

Claudia nodded. It had to be Chris. She'd have to caution him about looking in on the girls when she was working with them. He was a distraction the girls, and she, didn't need right now.

Claudia let the girls go at five o'clock and asked them all to come back in the late afternoon on Monday to practice together. She asked Nani Li'i to come in an hour early so they could work on her presentation. Claudia was going to have to do some shopping before the show the next weekend. She didn't have the outfit she wanted Nani Li'i to wear, but next year she certainly would include a design or two for the idea she had formed around the hula.

She opened the door to the suite and smelled something good. David was in the kitchen, cooking. She couldn't believe what she was seeing. He grinned at her as she came into the kitchen.

"Hi, babe."

He was clean-shaven and dressed in a T-shirt and shorts. She could smell the aftershave she had brought for him to use, and her heart spun. Just when she thought she could get over him, he did a complete about-face.

"What are you doing?" she asked, a little incredulously.

"I'm fixing us dinner."

"You're a wonder!"

"No. You are, and I want you back in my life for good."

"Oh, David, please don't start that again."

"I mean it, CJ. The leg is getting better, and I'm going to clean up my act and get off the stuff."

"Nothing would please me more, but don't make promises you can't keep."

He shut off the burner under the pan of stir-fry he was cooking and pulled it off the heat. With one hand on the counter to help him, he hopped on his good leg until he was standing in front of her.

"I intend to keep this one, babe, because I intend to keep you."

He took her in his arms and she let him, wanting this David more than she had ever wanted anyone. Wanting to believe he could change. Wanting to believe it could be like it had been on her trip to Hawaii after their first date at Cowboy Kapana's Bar. She had stayed with him after that assignment was over.

◆ ◆ ◆

When Claudia had been dismissed from the shoot, she thought about calling David, but it had been a brief thought. He had given her no indication he wanted to see her again. She took a taxi to the airport and flew to Honolulu. Getting a flight to New York took a little longer, but when she finally made it to her New York apartment, the light was flashing on her answering machine. She pushed the message button and smiled as she heard David's voice.

"Haole woman, why didn't you call me? I want to hear from you. You have my number. Call me."

She called him.

"Why didn't you call me, CJ?"

"I left rather suddenly."

"What do you mean, you left suddenly?"

"The shoot director called my room and you answered the phone. I got fired and sent back to New York."

He uttered a soft expletive and said, "CJ, you should have called me. You could have stayed with me for as long as you wanted."

"I didn't feel like I knew you well enough to impose on you."

"Listen, babe, You can call me any time, from anywhere, and I would come for you. Understand?"

His voice was an intimate whisper her whole body understood and responded to. "Yes, David."

"How about you coming just for me? Can you do that?"

"I haven't talked to anyone here yet. I'll know more after I talk to my agency."

"You do that, and call me. I've got you in my blood, haole woman. I've thought of nothing else but you since Sunday night."

"As soon as I know something, I'll call you."

She reported to her agency the next day. Cherise Morgan, the head of the agency, was out of town. It was several days before she was called in to see her agent. She waited nervously in the outer office until her agent's secretary told her she could go in.

Cherise looked up and smiled at Claudia as she entered. "Please sit down, CJ."

Claudia sat down. The smile had been genuine, and it helped ease Claudia's nervousness. She and Cherise had always had a good rapport. Her agent was someone Claudia admired and emulated. Cherise was a former model and had seen in Claudia the same qualities she possessed: elegance, poise, dependability, and professionalism. They had liked each other immediately. They looked enough alike to have been sisters, except Cherise was a good fifteen years older than her protégé.

"I've talked to the shoot director who dismissed you. She said you violated curfew, and when she called your room the next morning, a man answered. I'm surprised to hear that—especially about you, CJ. You have always maintained an impeccable reputation. I shouldn't have to tell you, because you should know this, but you were totally out of line. In her position, I would have dismissed you, too, if for no other reason than to make an example of you for the other girls.

"But in my position, what do I do with you? You are one of the best models this agency has, but if you get a reputation for this kind of thing, you're worth nothing to me. Now, I would like to think that this breach of contract will not happen again. I don't want you blackballed, CJ—you're too good for that. But you will be if you are sent home again. Do I make myself clear?"

"Yes. I understand and accept total responsibility for what happened, and it will never happen again. I promise."

Cherise Morgan's face softened, as did her tone of voice. "Was it the artist you met last year?"

"Yes."

"Is this serious, CJ?"

"He's a very interesting man. I think it could be very serious."

"How much time do you want me to schedule you for after the next shoot in Hawaii?"

"As much time as you can."

Cherise smiled, her eyebrows arching questioningly. "He must be a very good artist."

Claudia smiled back. "He's like no one I've ever met before."

"Just how much do you know about him? About his family? His friends?"

Claudia frowned. "I met his mother. His father died before David was born. David was raised in the small Hawaiian village where his mother's family lived. His grandparents helped raise him. He is a self-made man. He competed in the triathlon until he was injured in a hit and run accident. He's a gifted artist and seems to do well enough that he can help his mother." Claudia paused and frowned. "The one thing that bothers me is that he is using marijuana to alleviate his pain."

It was Cherise's turn to frown. She shook her head in dissent. "For God's sake, Claudia, you of all people should know better. You've seen enough druggies in this business that you should not think for a minute that you can change this man just because you love him. I will see that you get some time off, but you must promise me that you will not break the rules again."

Claudia nodded her agreement.

Claudia got a month off after her next shoot in Hawaii and spent the entire time with David. Those days had been paradise.

◆ ◆ ◆

Claudia struggled against David, pushing against him with both hands until he released her.

"Damn it, CJ. What the hell are you doing?" he demanded.

She retorted, "I should be asking you that. You tell me you are going to clean up your act, but you have been smoking, David. Just forget it until you can prove to me you've quit."

He gave her a pained look. "CJ, that was my last one. I made up my mind to quit, and I mean it. I want you in the worst way, babe—more than anything else."

"Then prove it by staying off the drugs. When you can do that, I'm willing to listen to you. Now go sit down, and I'll serve you dinner before it gets any colder."

On Monday morning, she began looking for the things she needed for Nani Li'i. She bought a length of material at a fabric store and started inquiring for a shop that specialized in the type of dress she had in mind for the girl to wear for the fashion show. She was told she could find what she was looking for across the island at Wailuku. She would have to go there on Tuesday and hope they had what she wanted.

When Nani Li'i came in to work with her on Monday afternoon, Claudia took the length of material she had bought, tucked it inside the waistband of her shorts, and told Nani Li'i to watch her demonstrate what she wanted her to do with the train of cloth. She turned on the music and moved in a slow, undulating hula down the runway, trailing the train and artfully flipping it from side to side as she moved. She faced one way and then the other, so she could be seen from both sides of the runway, as well as from straight ahead.

When she reached the end of the runway, Nani Li'i was smiling. "That was cool, but I won't ever be able to do that!"

"Yes, you can, and you will. There's just the two of us, and we are going to do this together until you get it. Now come up here and show me what you really can do."

"But what about that man?"

"Don't worry about Chris. If he comes in again, you tell me and I'll ask him to leave."

That seemed to satisfy her, and Claudia finished tucking the train into the waistband of Nani's shorts and started the music.

After an intense hour of working alone with the girl, Claudia felt they were getting somewhere. Nani was loosening up and beginning to dance like she meant it. She had trouble mastering the train, but

Claudia felt she would have it all together by the end of the week. She was smiling and confident when the rest of the girls showed up for practice.

On Tuesday morning, Claudia drove to Wailuku and found the shop she was looking for. They had exactly what she wanted: a beautiful satin gown with a train to fit Nani Li'i.

On her way back, she stopped at a flower shop in Lahaina to order the flowers she wanted for the day of the fashion show. Then she visited the local radio station to have the fashion show announced on the air, and she picked up the posters she would deliver to shops along Front Street the next morning.

She bought sandwiches and took them to her suite for lunch. David was out on the veranda, finishing a joint of marijuana. He must have heard her enter. He came into the kitchen, where she was pouring iced tea for their lunch.

"Did you get what you needed in Wailuku?"

"Yes. I got the perfect dress." She was happy with the way things were falling into place.

"Are you going to invite me to your show?"

"Of course, if you want to come."

"Sure. I'd like to see what excites you more than I can."

"Please, David, don't start that again."

He shrugged, dropped onto the chair at the bar, and took a long drink of tea as Claudia set a sandwich before him. He ate silently, avoiding her eyes. He was deliberately being difficult, and she counted the hours until the doctor's appointment on Friday.

Her afternoon session with Nani Li'i went well. The girl was beginning to have confidence in herself as she began catching on to dancing with the train. Claudia encouraged her. The more praise the girl got, the harder she tried and the better she did. Claudia was glowing with pride for the girl. Her instincts had been right. Beneath the shy, lumbering exterior, there was a beautiful, graceful young woman waiting to bloom.

On Thursday, Claudia held her last practice with the girls. At the end of the session, she sat them down and talked to them about what she expected from them on Friday.

"Okay, girls. This is it. I want you all back her by six o'clock tomorrow. At eight o'clock, we are going to have a dress rehearsal. I will have a sign up in the lobby tomorrow inviting anyone staying at the hotel to come watch. There will be posters going up along Front Street, and Henri has promised me a big sign on the sidewalk outside."

Young, excited faces looked at each other with mock panic. Claudia continued. "We will be in the ballroom at the end of the hall for tomorrow and Saturday afternoon. We will be able to use the dressing rooms and showers, so everyone plan on showering and washing your hair before the program tomorrow night. The same for Saturday. I will be there to help you with makeup and hair.

"The posters are on the table by the door. Each one of you can take one for a souvenir; more if you have someplace you can display them to advertise the show.

"Okay. That's it, unless you have some questions."

For once, there were no questions. Nervously, they trooped out of the conference room, and Claudia was alone. She felt a flutter in the pit of her stomach, too.

CHAPTER VII

Claudia called for her car to be brought to the lobby entrance. David's appointment was at nine o'clock. Silently, he made his way to the elevator with Claudia following, carrying the bag of clothes and necessities she had brought for him while he stayed with her. He had been giving her the silent treatment since Tuesday, and she felt a secret relief that the stress of having him with her would soon be over. It had been the antidote she needed to finally cure her of the love she had let fester in her since she had left him. She still cared for him, but now she felt compassion instead of the aching need of passion. She had been able to resist his ardor and her own, and had found peace with her decision.

The elevator doors opened when they reached the lobby. She held the door open until David maneuvered outside. Claudia followed and saw Chris come out of his office. David saw him, too, but Claudia kept right on walking, pretending not to notice the man who watched them so intently.

The doctor took the stitches out of the cut on David's face and exchanged the hard cast for a walking cast. Claudia breathed a sigh of relief when they were finally on their way to David's studio. He was silent until they got inside his backdoor.

"Well, babe, I guess I should thank you for taking pity on me."

"It wasn't pity, David."

He turned and looked at her with hurt in his eyes. "Then what was it, CJ?"

She shrugged. "Let's just say it was for old time's sake."

He freed himself of the crutches and took her in his arms. "Baby, don't leave me. I need you. We can make it be just like the old times again. We are so good together."

She resisted him, pushing against him as she protested, "No, David. I can't stay with you. I can't stand what you are doing to yourself."

"But I've been doing better. I've been leaving the hard stuff alone."

"It's not enough. If you want me in your life, you will have to quit it all."

He released her. "If you really loved me, you wouldn't ask me to give any of it up. You know I need it."

"I don't want this discussion again, David. I'm leaving now."

"It's that cop, isn't it?"

"I don't know what you're talking about."

"The guy at the hotel. The one you were with that night."

"You mean Chris? No. I haven't seen him since that night."

"Don't lie to me, Claudia. I saw how he looked at you back at the hotel."

"I'm not lying to you. There is no one else. I was still in love with you. I haven't wanted anyone else."

"Then why aren't you wanting me now? I love you, damn it."

"I've told you why. Now I'm leaving. Good-bye." She reached for the door, but he wasn't about to give up and let her go.

"When did you tell me you were going back to New York?"

"In a couple of weeks. I'll take you to the doctor if you want me to. If you need anything else between now and then, you can give me a call."

"Okay."

She had never seen him so pathetic looking. It made her want to take him in her arms and tell him everything was going to be all right, but she knew she couldn't. It would be playing into the guilt trip he was trying to lay on her. The silent treatment hadn't worked, and neither would this. She said, "Take care of yourself, David."

He nodded, and she was out the door. She didn't look back.

She was starving by the time she got back to the hotel. She had been under so much stress with David and the show that she had eaten only out of necessity. She crossed the threshold into the hotel lobby. She looked at the mirrored wall and waved. Chris came out the door, and she stopped, holding out her hands, wrists together. He laughed as he stopped in front of her, taking her hands in his. "You're under arrest, Bonnie. Where's Clyde?"

"We've split up. You'll never take him alive."

The smile left his eyes and a strange look crossed his face. He released her hands. "What happened?"

"Can I tell you over lunch? I'm starved."

"Sure."

They were seated in the garden area by the hostess, who wore a beautiful island print muumuu and a fragrant plumeria lei. The tables in the garden area were arranged among plantings of palms, hibiscus, anthurium, birds of paradise, and ginger. Recirculating streams of water wound through the area under bridges and over small waterfalls, creating a subtle, soothing atmosphere. Claudia loved the concept. For stormy days and pineapple mists, the magic of specially designed translucent, waterproof panels covered the open area, providing light and allowing uninterrupted use of the entire area. Their waitress, wearing a tropical print sarong, came with water and took their order.

Chris, apparently unable to keep his curiosity under control, asked, "Where's Keanu?"

"I took him to the doctor today. They removed the hard cast and put him in a walking cast. I'm done being his nurse."

Chris gave her another centerfold grin and said, "You don't know how happy I am to hear that. Henri has been giving me a hard time about Keanu. We were alerted to the fact that he was in your room the first day he was there. The desk was getting calls from people who were smelling marijuana. We alerted housekeeping to be on the lookout for the source. One of the maids did come to my office after she had finished cleaning your room and reported that there was a man in your suite and he was smoking marijuana while she cleaned your room. She also found needles and syringes in the wastebasket. It put me between a rock and a hard spot. If I reported it you know what would hit the fan. Then Henri found out about it and, as you might guess, he was upset. I did my best to convince him that things would work out and they have."

Claudia reached across the table and took Chris's hand, her eyes misty with tears of gratitude. "Thank you so much, Chris. I'm so sorry to have put you through this." She paused, realizing just how much she'd had to lose if Henri had wanted to make a case over David. It would have ruined her and what she was trying to do for the girls she was working with. "I just didn't know what else to do."

Chris put his other hand over the top of hers, smiled and asked, "I hope this means you'll have time for some vacation after you're done with the fashion show?"

"Yes."

"Good. Maybe I could interest you in going sailing with me."

"I'm afraid not. I get seasick on the dock."

"Well, how about sunrise on Haleakala?"

She laughed. "We'll see."

"Okay, then. What would you like to do?"

"All I want to do right now is just not have anything to do. Sleep in, lay around the pool, go swimming, read a good book, and go to bed."

"I'd be interested in doing that."

Claudia's cheeks reddened as she realized what she had said. She was saved from trying to explain herself by the arrival of their lunch.

During lunch, Claudia asked Chris, "David acted like he knew you. Do you live here year-round?"

"Yes. I was born and raised on Oahu. But when I got out of school, the first job I could get was on Maui, so I've been here ever since."

"Do you still have family living on Oahu?"

"Yes, the folks are still there. My sis married a haole and moved to Washington State."

She frowned at him. "Aren't you a haole, too?"

"Well, yes, but not in the same way. I'm the second generation of my family to be born in Hawaii, so I consider myself a native of Hawaii. But not everyone does."

"So your grandparents originally came here to live?"

"Yes. My grandfather was in the construction business. They needed construction workers back then, so he and my grandmother came here thinking they would stay as long as grandfather was making big money. They never went back to the mainland, except for visits. My father was born here, but he went to college on the mainland and brought home a haole bride. The rest is history."

"Did you go to college here, or on the mainland?"

Between bites, he answered, "Mainland. I wasn't anxious to go, but the folks insisted on it. They felt I should experience the mainland in case I got island fever at some point in my life. But I never have, and I doubt I ever will."

"And you didn't bring back a bride?"

He gave her a soft, tender kind of smile and shook his head. "No. I wanted to find someone who felt like I do about these islands and wouldn't be unhappy spending the rest of her life here."

Their waitress came by their table and asked, "Will there be anything else I can get you?"

Claudia answered, "No. I need to get to work. Please put this on my bill. Room 405."

The waitress gave a nod and smiled, saying, "Please come again."

Chris protested. "I thought I was taking you to lunch?"

"I asked you. Remember?"

"I'll leave the tip." He pulled a five-dollar bill out of his billfold and stood up. "Thanks for lunch."

"My pleasure."

"Going to your room?"

"No. I need to check on the ballroom and see how things are shaping up there."

"Okay. I'll see you later."

Claudia watched him walk toward the lobby. She turned in the opposite direction, thinking it had been a pleasure to be with him now that she had finally gotten David out of her system. Chris seemed to be a really nice guy and appeared to be totally nonthreatening. She was beginning to feel comfortable with him. He was easy to talk to and good to look at. Maybe he was just the kind of safe haven she needed after David. She smiled all the way to the ballroom.

The hotel staff was almost finished getting the runway ready and the chairs in place for the dress rehearsal. She checked out the sound equipment and made sure the music was in the machine and ready to play. Everything looked like it would be perfect. She went to her display room, took all the clothing she wasn't going to use, and began packing it into her trunks. The empty racks were also broken down and packed into their boxes. When she was done, only the clothes that were going to be used in the show were left on three racks.

She returned to the ballroom and got two of the staff to move the racks into the dressing rooms behind the ballroom stage. Once that was done, she concentrated on getting every outfit put together with the accessories. She visualized the girls who would be wearing the outfits. She would need to go back to her suite to get the makeup kits she needed to finish the girls before the show. She went over everything again to make sure she had all she needed before she left the dressing room for her suite.

CHAPTER VIII

Claudia was in the ballroom, making sure every detail was perfect, when the first group of her girls arrived. She went with them to the dressing room. When they were done with their showers, Claudia had hair dryers and makeup ready for each girl on the dressing room counters. They were thrilled and excited with the personal attention she gave them. By the time Claudia got done with them, they glowed as they admired themselves and each other in the mirrored walls.

Nani Li'i was the last one to come in, and Claudia was relieved to see her. She was getting worried that Nani wouldn't show up at all. The rest of the girls could finish getting ready without her, and Claudia devoted her full attention to Nani Li'i. Wrapped in a beach towel and with a towel around her hair, Claudia took her to a station at the dressing table. She began by putting conditioner on the girl's thick, heavy, black hair. It kinked as badly as Claudia's when it was wet. Claudia wanted Nani's hair to flow in gentle waves over her back and shoulders. Once she had achieved that look, she went on to apply a soft glow of color to Nani's cheeks and a pearly luminescence to her eyelids. Then she defined her lips and added the deep, rose pink color of torch ginger to her lips. The effect was stunning, and the girls who were watching the process began to ooh and ahh. Nani smiled at the mirror image of herself. She was beautiful.

Claudia squeezed the girl's shoulder with approval and said, "You are lovely, Nani. Now get your first outfit on. It's time for me to hit the stage. Any last-minute questions?" They looked at each other, giggled with nervousness, but shook their heads. "Good. Now just remember, keep focused and smile."

Claudia left the dressing room and climbed the stairs to the stage. She was gratified to see there were people seated in the ballroom. Some of them would be the parents and families of the girls, but there were also some hotel guests, and Henri was seated at the end of the runway. Claudia picked up the microphone and began the introduction to her program.

When she turned on the music, it was the cue for the first model to come on stage. She had chosen Mikko as her first model. The girl was a natural, poised and confident for her years. Her enthusiasm and ability to be a cheerleader for the rest of the girls would keep the show from breaking down.

Mikko came out of the wings wearing a bathing suit under a gauzy cover-up just translucent enough to be provocative. Her small, perfectly formed body and delicately exotic features made her first choice for the bathing suits in Claudia's line, and she executed the runway better than any of the girls, doing as well as anyone at seductively taking off the cover-up to reveal her exquisite body.

When Mikko turned to strut back up the runway, there was a round of applause, and Claudia's confidence soared. She began to relax, and from that moment on she felt no stress. She just enjoyed watching her girls achieve what she had been training them to do.

At nine o'clock, Nani Li'i stepped onto the runway. She was stunning: a vision in a pale pink satin *holoku* with sleeves fitted to the elbow, then flared to the wrist and finished with a narrow lace ruffle. The neck of the dress was open to just above her breasts in a design called sweetheart similar to the curves at the top of a heart, with the same lace ruffle in a paler shade of pink than the color of the gown. The dress was fitted to her hips and flared into a full train with more ruffling on the hem.

A ring of white flowers graced Nani's dark hair, which glistened blue-black in the spotlight and fell in deep, soft waves over her shoulders and down her back. Her feet were bare, and she moved down the runway to "The Hawaiian Wedding Song" in a graceful hula. The train of the dress flowing behind her seemed to have a life of its own as it moved from side to side in perfect rhythm with every elegant, flowing turn and step. She seemed to have been transformed into a weightless, lyrical beauty, moving with such effortless grace she seemed to float.

Claudia stood off to the side of the stage behind a wooden podium, glowing with pride at the hypnotic effect the young Hawaiian girl was having on the audience. All eyes were on the girl, and there was no sound except the music.

When Nani Li'i finished her dance at the end of the runway, posed in a kneeling curtsy, the audience remained hushed. When she regally rose and turned to walk back up the runway, Claudia saw Chris as he stood near the rear of the auditorium. He started clapping. It brought the audience out of its trance, and they rose to their feet and clapped with him.

Claudia came from behind the podium, took the girl in her arms, and hugged her. Then she turned her around, and they bowed together as the audience continued to applaud them. Claudia motioned the rest of the girls out, and they came onto the stage to a renewed round of applause, walking down the runway to greet their families, exhilarated by what they had done.

The lights in the ballroom came on. Chris was opening the ballroom doors. He stepped aside as the room began to empty and moved down the aisle against the crowd. The girls disappeared down the runway toward the stage and the dressing room to change. Claudia came down the stage steps and was stopped by Henri just as Chris reached them.

"Oh, my dear Claudia! You have worked a miracle here. These young ladies were so ... *magnifique*! I compliment you. You are truly a woman of these islands to have designed these clothes and learned the expression of the islands in the hula and given these girls an experience they can all be proud of," he stopped, overcome with emotion. Then continued, "I want to make this an annual event. Let the other hotels have their luaus—we will have our fashion show!" He took her by the shoulders and kissed both her cheeks.

She laughed happily. "Thank you, Henri. I am so pleased you liked it. I enjoyed doing it. The girls did such a wonderful job. I really would like to do it again, but I'll have to see what happens. But please, let's make tentative plans to do it about this time next year."

"Wonderful! Come into my office before you leave, and we will look at the calendar for next year."

He took her hand and kissed it, then turned snappily and scurried past Chris and up the aisle. Claudia turned her eyes on Chris, seeing his appreciative smile. "Well, now what do you think?"

"I couldn't agree with Henri more. I think you worked a miracle. I guess I owe you dinner." His eyes told her his appreciation wasn't just for what she had accomplished, but for her as well.

Her heart was warmed by the look in his eyes, but it worried her, too. She wasn't ready for another relationship. She didn't really know him. Yes, he had answered her questions, but what did she really know besides the fact that he was a hotel security man and had been born on the islands? When she summed it up, it wasn't enough. Especially after David.

She laughed and said, "I don't remember anything about dinner."

"I'll take you out to dinner anyway. How did you do what you did with Nani Li'i? She was absolutely stunning. I can't believe she's the same girl I saw a week ago."

"She did it. She just needed someone to believe in her and encourage her. She was beautiful, wasn't she?"

"Yes. And so is her teacher."

"Thank you. How much of the program did you see?"

"I just got here when Nani Li'i was on the runway. I'll try to get in and see the whole thing tomorrow. Then I want to take you out to dinner."

She shook her head. "I've got a lot to do after the show. I'd better not commit to anything."

"How about if I stick around and help you?"

"Are you sure? You must have better things to do."
"Right now I can't think of any."

◆ ◆ ◆

The Saturday fashion show drew more of a crowd. There were few empty seats in the ballroom when Claudia stepped out of the wings and took her place behind the podium to introduce the show. She was wearing a silk dress in shades of turquoise and blue. A lovely lei of white plumeria completed her outfit. She spotted Chris in a seat about halfway down the runway. He was sitting with Henri.

If anything, the fashion show went off even better than the dress rehearsal had. The crowd was a mix of tourists, family, friends, and classmates of the girls, and locals. There was a lot of enthusiasm for seeing hometown girls doing something special. By the end of the show, when Nani Li'i was to do the closing number, Claudia felt radiant. All she had to do was look at Chris to know what kind of impression she was making.

Nani Li'i took to the runway like a seasoned trouper. Claudia had seen vestiges of shyness and reserve in her performance during the dress rehearsal, but now there was only a fleeting moment of stage fright as she saw the crowded room. A cheer went up from her family as she assumed her opening pose and held it until the audience quieted. The room lights dimmed, the spotlights enveloped her in ethereal light, and the music began.

From somewhere within, this island girl drew out of herself all the grace, beauty, innocence, and sensuousness of her ancestors, and she was transformed into something magical. Except for the music and the soft swishing of the satin train as it swirled provocatively around her, there was complete silence in the ballroom. She swayed, keeping rhythm with her beautiful, long-fingered, expressive hands. Her face was radiant and enraptured by what she was experiencing as she discovered herself. Claudia knew the girl would never be the same after this experience.

The music ended, and Nani Li'i knelt at the end of the runway, absorbing the adulation as the admiring people in the ballroom gave her a standing ovation. She rose with newfound dignity and regal poise. She looked like she believed she was descended from Hawaiian royalty.

Claudia reached into the podium, retrieved a lei of fragrant white plumeria, and placed it over Nani's head as the girl reached the stage. She kissed her cheeks and turned, holding her hand. They bowed together to the applause. Claudia motioned the rest of the girls on stage, and they came strutting out like seasoned models to the cheers of their families and friends.

It took an hour for Claudia to finally finish talking to all the people who wanted to compliment her on the show and what she had done with the girls.

At the end of the long line of people, Chris was waiting. He smiled at her and shook his head in wonder. "I'm really impressed, Claudia."

"Thank you." She smiled back. "I think they did a marvelous job."

"More than marvelous. And so are you."

"You flatter me. The girls had to want to do it, or nothing I did would have mattered."

"You know what I was thinking while I watched them?"

"What?"

"What about giving some boys a chance to try this next year?"

She looked at him thoughtfully, envisioning Chris on the runway. He certainly was model material. He had everything a male model should have: a great face, great hair, and great legs. And no doubt the parts of him she hadn't seen were just as well-sculpted as the parts she saw. With a mischievous smile, she said, "I think it's a great idea. I think I'd like to start with you."

He laughed but said, "No way! I meant boys."

"What if I train you to train them?"

"I think I'm going to be sorry I mentioned this. Hadn't we better do what you need to do so I can take you out for dinner?"

"I need to change first. Give me a few minutes."

The light on Claudia's phone was blinking when she opened the door to her suite. She called the hotel desk for the message, and they gave her David's telephone number. He answered after several rings.

"Hello, David. I got your message. Is there something wrong?"

"Hi, baby. There's nothing wrong that you couldn't take care of. Come on over, and I'll prove it to you."

"Is this what you called to tell me?"

"That and the fact that I'm out food. Do you have time to take me out to get some groceries?"

"When do you want to go?"

"Now would be a good time."

She sighed. "I can't come now. How about tomorrow? Do you have anything at all to eat?"

"Not a damn thing. What are you doing now? Aren't you done with the fashion show?"

"Yes, but I have to get everything out of the ballroom today. Can I come get you later this evening?"

"Sure, babe. I'll see you later."

Claudia hung up the phone and frowned. She should have checked to see if he had anything to eat when she took him home. But he would have found some other excuse to call her. She should have known. As long as she was here, he was not going to leave her alone. With a sigh, she went to change her clothes.

She returned to the ballroom.

Chris said, "Is there something wrong?"

"I'm sorry I kept you waiting, but I had a message light on my phone. It's David. He wants me to take him grocery shopping tonight. May I have a rain check on dinner?"

A frown crossed Chris's face before he said, "Sure." He shrugged his shoulders and gave her a half-hearted smile. "Well, we better get started with your cleanup so you can get him taken care of."

She placed her hand on his arm. "Chris, this isn't fair to you. I can't expect you to help me under the circumstances."

He placed his hand on top of hers and smiled lopsidedly. "Hey, I'm not complaining. Now quit trying to discourage me, and let's get the job done."

She smiled back at him. "Okay. You know what P. T. Barnum said?"

"I think it was something about one being born every minute."

She laughed and withdrew her hand. "You said it."

He helped her pack up everything the girls had not taken with them after the show. Claudia had given the girls their choice of the clothes they wanted from those they had modeled, plus the makeup, hair dryers, and anything else she had provided for them at her expense. She had even arranged for the show to be taped by a professional video studio, and each girl would have a keepsake tape of the show. She had thought of everything to make the experience a good memory for the girls who had participated.

When everything was boxed up and ready to be transferred back to the small conference room, Chris borrowed a luggage cart from the lobby, and they moved everything except the few things Claudia needed. Chris helped her carry those to her room.

It was the first time he'd been inside her suite. He whistled. "Nice."

She turned to look at him. "You've never been in one of these suites before?"

"No." His forehead creased in a frown. "I think I've underestimated you."

Claudia looked puzzled. "What do you mean?"

He made a sweeping motion with his arm. "This suite, the fashion show—what you did for those girls, the clothes you design and wear, it all tells me you are way out of my class."

Claudia placed her hand on his arm and smiled, "You didn't hear the speech I gave to the girls. I wasn't born with money. I came from an ordinary working class family. I just got lucky."

He smiled at that. "Oh, I think it was more than just luck."

She nodded, "It took hard work and taking some risks."

He nodded and changed the subject. "What are you going to do with all this stuff? Ship it back to the mainland?"

"Yes. Unfortunately, what comes over has to go back."

"It wouldn't have to if you lived here."

"I've thought about that. It appeals to me, but I don't know just yet if I could swing it on these island lines alone. Maybe in a few years it might be feasible."

"How about trying it for just a few months at a time?"

"Maybe. I'll have to see how this year's sales go. Then I might consider it. It would be hard to change right now because of my other lines of clothing. I'd have to find a company to do the actual assembly of the clothes, or I might even have to set up my own production company. In that case, I would have to find someone to do the fabrics. There's a lot involved in moving my base of operations."

He nodded. "Well, it was just a thought."

"Believe me, I have thought about it, too."

He smiled. "Well, I'd better not keep you. May I give you a call tomorrow?"

"Sure. And thanks for the help. I really appreciate it."

He stood for a moment, indecision in his eyes. Claudia wondered if he was going to kiss her and her lips parted expectantly.

He shrugged and said, "Anytime," and turned to go.

CHAPTER IX

Claudia pulled her car in behind David's Jeep and got out. She knocked on David's door.

His voice answered her, "Come in; it's open."

She opened the door, smelled the distinctive odor of marijuana, and frowned. David appeared at the top of the stairs, dressed only in a towel wrapped around his hips. His hair was wet, and water still ran down his chest.

"Hi, babe. Want to come upstairs and see my etchings?"

"No, I do not want to come upstairs. I thought you needed groceries."

"I do, but I need you worse, baby." He removed the towel from around his hips and started drying himself, revealing all of his body to her.

"If you're that desperate, why don't you call Rosa? I'm sure she'd be glad to come help you out of your misery."

He grinned, his white teeth flashing in his dark face. "She can't hold a candle to you, baby. Besides, she's gone. You're all I have left."

"Well, I'm sorry to hear that. Now get dressed and get down here if you want me to take you shopping."

"Just a little bitchy today, huh?"

"Look, David. I might have had something better I wanted to do with my time. Now go get dressed."

He disappeared, but his voice came down to her with an edge to it. "You're not seeing the cop, are you?"

"If you mean Chris, yes. He asked me out to dinner tonight." She wandered toward the front of the studio to see what new paintings he might have finished since she had last been there. There was little evidence he had painted anything recently. She was not impressed with the one painting that was completed. It was a departure from what he had done in the past. He was trying to emulate some of the more popular artists, whose work hung in almost every art gallery in Lahaina.

In the last two decades, Lahaina had become an artist's town. The shops along Front Street had been converted into galleries to show the wealth of paintings produced by the new preservationist artists, whose themes centered around the sea and sea life, and whales in particular. David's painting featured a whale in the act of flipping her newborn calf into the air to stimulate it to breathe. It was a good painting but not as distinctive as his usual style.

David's style emulated that of Herb Kane, another well-known Hawaiian artist. Kane's paintings depicted scenes of ancient Hawaiian legends; kings, battles, religious ceremonies, and gods and goddesses. They revealed the old Hawaiian ways and the evolving Hawaiian society after the first white missionaries and ranchers came. They were beautiful paintings, filled with the rich, vibrant color of the islands and their native people. Her favorite Kane painting, one of a beautiful Hawaiian girl dancing the hula, had inspired the idea for Nani Li'i in the fashion show.

She heard David coming down the steps. He was saying, "I'm warning you, CJ. You better stay away from him. He's big trouble."

"And just who are you to tell me who I can see?"

He stopped in front of her at the foot of the stairs. "Didn't you tell me I was the only man you ever wanted, and if you ever looked at another man, to remind you there could never be another man for you?"

Sadly, she admitted, "I remember."

"Then come back to me. You're the only woman I want. With your help, I could get my life back on track."

She sighed. No matter how much she wanted to believe him—wanted their relationship to be as it had been before the heavy drug use—she knew it wasn't possible. "No, David. It won't work. You have to do it all by yourself. Now, do you have a list of groceries you want to get?"

"Sure. I got it memorized. Let's go."

She drove him to the nearest grocery store, a few blocks away.

"How about I buy you something to eat, since neither one of us has had dinner?"

"I really didn't want to spend that much time."

"What's your hurry? The cop waiting for you?"

"No. No one is waiting for me. I just don't see any point in us being together."

"Okay, babe. Have it your way."

They did his shopping, and Claudia picked some things up for herself. They drove back to his studio in silence. She pulled in behind his Jeep before he finally said something.

"I've got another favor to ask you, CJ. I need to go to Wailua tomorrow, and you're the only one I can depend on to get me there."

"Did it ever occur to you I might have something else to do?" There was an edge to her voice.

He put his hand behind her and caressed her neck. "This is important, baby. You know I wouldn't ask unless it was."

"How important?"

"Well, it's for Rosa. She needs some more clothes. It's not as warm on the mainland as she thought it would be."

"Why can't Rosa's family mail them? They have to come down to Paia once in a while, don't they? Why do you have to make a special trip?"

"That's not all. The day of the accident at Hard Rock, I took pictures of her for her portfolio. I never got them done because of being laid up. Now they're done, and I've got to get them to her. She needs them to get into this modeling school. I told her I'd take care of it for her. That's the least I could do."

Claudia frowned. She didn't believe for a moment that Rosa had the dedication necessary to make it through modeling school. Rosa had barely made it through high school. She could believe Rosa had gone to California in hopes of becoming a model, or even a movie star. She was an attractive girl, even pretty. But basically, the girl lacked class. And that lack of class would mean rejection. Claudia hated to think where rejection would lead a girl like Rosa, who was too immature to realize there were people who would take advantage of her.

Claudia sighed and gave in. She had no plans for Sunday. She might as well take David to Wailua and get it over with. "All right. What time do you want me to pick you up?"

"As early as you want to. I'll be ready."

"Okay."

He leaned over and kissed her on the cheek. "Want a drink?"

"No thanks." She opened her door, reached in the backseat of the convertible for his groceries, and headed for the backdoor of the studio.

◆ ◆ ◆

Claudia liked going to Wailua and Keanae, where David's mother lived. It was a Hawaii few tourists saw. The natives in the villages subsisted on what they could raise, catch out of the ocean, or hunt on the slopes of Haleakala. Life there was much like it had been before the turn of the twentieth century.

The road to Wailua and to Hana had had only minor improvements since the last time she had driven it. The road followed the rugged slopes of Haleakala, twisting and turning in and out of gorges, where sparkling mountain streams flowed under narrow, single-lane bridges and plunged toward the ocean hundreds of feet below, creating spectacular waterfalls.

Around every curve—and there were many of them—there were views of the ocean or rain forest. The tops of African tulip trees blazed with flame-colored flowers at road level from the gorges, and tiny sprays of orchids clung to the seeping, black lava cliffs on the passenger side of the car. Claudia had to take Dramamine to keep from getting carsick. Wailua was more than halfway to Hana. Once she was on the Hana Highway, it was a two-hour drive.

They turned off the main road and onto the one-lane road leading down into the little village of Wailua. It was on a sloping bench of land between the highway and the ocean. It had been raining on this side of the island, and the humidity was high in this sheltered village, quickly making Claudia feel sticky in the heavy, muggy stillness. Almost as quickly, the insects found her, and she was glad she had remembered the second most important thing besides the Dramamine: her insect repellent.

She stopped in front of the wooden frame house where Rosa's family lived. It was like most of the native houses. It had a rusting, corrugated metal roof. It had been built on posts to raise it off the ground. Latticework enclosed the area between the house and the ground, though sections were broken or missing altogether. When Claudia stopped the car in the dirt driveway behind Puna's rusting four-wheel-drive pickup, several hound dogs came yelping out from underneath the house. The dogs were used to hunt wild pigs and feral goats living on the slopes of the mountain above the village.

Puna, a shorter, darker-skinned, and heavier man than David, came out of the house wearing nothing but a pair of cutoffs. David waved. Puna yelled at the dogs, and they quieted. He came to the car and looked at Claudia with distrust. "Why you bring her here?"

"Come on, Puna. How else was I supposed to get here?"

Puna grunted. "I'll get da suitcase." He turned and stalked back into the house.

Claudia had never felt comfortable in Puna's presence. He disliked every haole who set foot on his island. He made no exceptions, not even for Claudia, though Puna knew how David felt about her. David accepted it and shrugged it off with, "That's just how he is."

Puna returned with the suitcase and ordered Claudia, "Open da trunk."

She frowned at his disdain, but pulled the trunk release lever. Puna set the case inside and closed the trunk. He came to David's side of the car and said, "We gonna be up back side huntin' pigs on Wednesday if you wanna come up."

David nodded. "Yeah, I want to get some pictures while CJ is still here to drive me up. I'll see you then."

Claudia started the engine, furious at David for making plans without even asking her first. Puna grunted again. He stood with his arms folded across his barrel chest and watched Claudia back out onto the road.

As soon as they were back on the highway, Claudia said, "It was nice of you to ask me if I was available Wednesday before you made your plans."

"I meant to, but you were so damn testy last night I thought I'd wait until today."

"We've been driving for three hours, David. Why did you wait until we got to Puna's before saying anything?"

"I'm sorry. Must have slipped my mind."

"It appears a lot of things have slipped your mind."

"Just what do you mean by that?" There was an edge to his voice.

"I looked around your studio last night. You aren't working on anything. And the one new painting I saw isn't your style. What's going on?"

"Have you forgotten I've had a broken ankle, and I had to get Rosa's pictures done?"

"You haven't painted for months, David. And why are you trying to paint like everyone else? There's too many sea-life, save-the-whales pictures now. What is wrong with what you were doing?"

"Economics, babe. The tourists want whales. So I decided to try to give 'em whales."

"That doesn't explain why you haven't painted anything in weeks."

"When you left me, I lost the enthusiasm to paint."

Claudia believed at least part of his statement might be true. He could have been that broken up over her leaving. He had loved her. David was a passionate man. He could be moody and quick to anger, but she thought it more likely he had gone on a binge of drinking and drugs and was unable to paint. "I'm truly sorry, David, if my leaving had anything to do with you not painting—if I am really to blame. I didn't want to hurt you in any way, especially your art. You have a special gift, David. I hate to see you waste it on doing something everyone else is doing."

"I have to do something to earn a living. If painting what I love doesn't sell, then I've got to try something that will."

"I understand that, David. But don't give up the other paintings. The part of you that does them is the best—the most inspired—part of you. I know you need to do something that sells, but you haven't been painting at all."

"How do you know what I've been doing or what I've been going through since you left me? We were good together, and you destroyed that. You destroyed me!"

Tears brimmed in Claudia's eyes, but she fought them back. He wanted her to feel guilty. He wanted her to feel sorry enough to come back to him. She couldn't let herself fall into his trap. If David was destroyed, it was by his own hand: a drink at a time, a joint at a time, or a needle or line at a time. Softly, she protested. "No, David. I won't take the blame for what you are doing to yourself. You were destroying yourself while I was with you. That's why I left you. You can't blame the drinking and the drugs on me."

"Forget it. You don't understand how things are."

He turned his head away from her, and she welcomed the silence. The last thing she wanted to do was argue with him. They had argued too much already.

She pulled up behind his Jeep and broke the silence. "What time do you want me to be here Wednesday?"

"I thought you weren't going to take me."

"I didn't say that. I am upset because you didn't tell me about it first, but I'll take you if you are sincere about doing a photo shoot for a painting."

"Yeah. I want to do a painting on wild pig hunting."

"Okay. I told you I would help you out as long as I was here. I won't break my promise. What time do you want me to pick you up?"

"I'd like to get up there by noon. Puna will be up there at first light, and if I know Puna, they'll have something before noon."

"Okay. I'll pick you up by nine." She popped the trunk lid and got out of the car. She lifted Rosa's suitcase out of the trunk and carried it inside for David.

"Thanks for everything, babe."

Claudia nodded and said, "I'll see you Wednesday."

The message light was blinking on her phone when she got back to her suite. She called the front desk and got the message that Chris had called, but he left no number. She was disappointed. She really had wanted to do something with him. She went into her bedroom, undressed, and went into the bathroom to take a shower. It felt good, even soothing, to let the water pour over her head, over her shoulders, and down her body. It was like a caress, and it brought a longing that had remained unfulfilled since she had broken up with David. She moved her hands down over her breasts, feeling the need stirring in her, and across the flat, firm surface of her abdomen to her thighs. She opened her eyes, feeling tears gathering in her throat. Her heart yearned in anguish between her full, aching breasts.

When she stepped out of the shower, the phone was ringing. Wrapping the towel around her dripping body, she went to the bedside phone and picked it up. "Hello?"

"Hi."

It was Chris, and Claudia smiled into the phone. "Hi. I'm sorry I missed you. I would've called, but you didn't leave a number."

"Is everything okay?"

"Yes. I'm sorry about today. I had to take David down to Wailua to pick up something. I didn't know about it until last night."

"No problem. Have you had anything to eat yet?"

"No."

"I'm just a couple of blocks away. If you want to have dinner with me, I can be there in a few minutes."

"Sure. But don't hurry. I just got out of the shower."

"If I'd known that, I wouldn't have called first."

Claudia laughed, feeling the ache move downward at his evocative words. "I'll see you in a few minutes."

Claudia was still blow-drying her hair when she heard Chris knock on the door. She went to the door, completely naked beneath the terrycloth robe she had wrapped around herself. Her heart was pounding with expectancy when she opened the door. He gave her a tender smile, and the subtle scent of his aftershave drifted provocatively to her. She felt a raw, urgent need engulf her. She looked at him expectantly, her lips parted, her breathing shallow. She stepped aside, let him come in, and closed the door.

Claudia didn't move and didn't speak. Chris turned around and said in a husky whisper, "Claudia?"

She moved then, coming to stand so close to him she could feel the warmth of his breath as she said, "I want you to make love to me."

He took her hands and gently answered, "No, Claudia. No matter how much I would like to, I think it would be a mistake for me to take advantage of what you are feeling right now. I wouldn't like myself afterward, and you wouldn't, either. I want to be more to you than a substitute for David Keanu. I want more than your body; I want your heart."

She lowered her eyes and withdrew her hands from his. "You're right. This is a mistake. Forget it." She brushed by him and went into the bedroom.

"Claudia. Wait. Let's talk about this." He followed her. She didn't respond. As he reached the bedroom door, she closed the bathroom door behind her. "Claudia, I'm sorry. I didn't handle this very well.

Please, come talk to me. I want to help you, but I've got to know what's wrong. Please, Claudia."

Claudia, her face twisted with anguish, couldn't answer.

"Claudia, I don't know what to say. I know you are hurting. I want to be the one to hold you and comfort you, if you want me to. I still want to take you to dinner. Or I can bring dinner up, if you want. I'm going to let myself out and go down to my office. If you want to talk this out, give me a call. Please, Claudia. I want to help you through this."

Claudia, leaning her head against the bathroom door in agony, heard Chris leave. She opened the door and fell facedown on the bed. She buried her face in her pillow and cried. With the release of tears, she made a decision. In the morning, she would call and see how soon she could get a flight to New York.

CHAPTER X

Claudia awoke at dawn, calmer, but still feeling humiliated by what she had asked Chris to do. The compulsion she had felt was foreign to her nature. It distressed her. She worried about what was happening to her. She had never felt so out of control. Though she felt less shame than she'd felt yesterday after Chris had left, she still felt it. She would not be able to face him again. Her last contact with him was indelibly printed in her memory. She saw the tenderness in his eyes, felt the warm compassion in his hands as they held hers, and heard the gentle honesty in his voice as he refused her.

She rose and went to shower and dress for the task she had to complete. She made breakfast from food she had left in her refrigerator. Before nine o'clock, she was in one of the smaller conference rooms, where they had stored her trunks until the freight company came for them. She made sure they were all secure, pasted new labels on the trunks, and had them ready to go in an hour.

Back in her room, she called the airline to see if she could reschedule her flight. She was given a new departure date for Friday. Only a few minutes after she hung up the phone, it rang. She knew it was Chris and didn't answer it. There was nothing she could say to him.

She fixed lunch in her suite and waited for the freight people. She jumped when someone knocked at her door. Before she opened it, she looked through the security peephole to make sure it wasn't Chris. It was the men to get her trunks. She wrote them a check and took them down to the room where the trunks and crates were stored. They began loading them onto hand trucks. She half expected Chris to show up at the door of the room, but he didn't, and she felt relieved. She just couldn't face him, not now, not ever.

She spent Tuesday shopping up and down both sides of Front Street. She had to buy gifts for her family and staff, and she took her time visiting every shop and gallery and otherwise losing herself in the tourist crowd walking the streets of Lahaina. She was beginning to look forward to Wednesday.

She arose early on Wednesday and dressed in shorts for her drive around the back side of Haleakala on the Kula-Pilani Highway. It would be a long drive, and it could get hot once they reached the barren, black fields of lava on the narrow, unimproved highway past Ulupalakua and the Tedeschi Winery. She had packed a lunch in a small foam cooler and used ice from the icemaker in her refrigerator to keep things cool.

She was at David's studio before nine o'clock. She knocked on his backdoor. It opened almost immediately.

"Hi, CJ. I'm almost ready."

He was gathering his equipment together on a table and putting it into bags. As he filled each bag, Claudia put it in the trunk of her car. He was zipping the last one closed when she came back inside the studio.

"I think I have it all now. Let's go."

She loaded the last bag into the car, and they were on their way. The drive through the Maui upcountry was as unique as the drive to Hana, with its own special climate and culture. Upcountry was somewhere between the near-desert climate of Lahaina and the rainforest climate of Hana. Huge eucalyptus and ironwood trees lined the lush pastures, where herds of cattle and dairy cows grazed, intermixed with truck gardens raising the vegetables feeding Maui and its ever-increasing number of tourists. Nurseries raised flowers for leis and exotic bouquets for shipping all over the world. On the west-facing slope of the mountain were residential communities with churches, schools, and views that spanned the isthmus between the two mountain masses that formed the island of Maui.

Past the ranch and winery, the road narrowed as it curved around to the south side of Haleakala, leaving behind the pastures and forested areas and passing into a drier, more desolate landscape formed of lava flows. The last lava flow happened in 1790. It was still a black, raw scar writhing its way down the mountain to the ocean at La Perouse Bay. More ancient flows were covered with thick, low brush, providing both forage and cover for the wild pigs and feral goats. A few hardy homesteaders, predominately of Hawaiian ancestry, eked out an existence here. They had no electric power, except from generators, and used bottled water or rainwater for drinking, bathing, and watering small garden plots and livestock.

David was saying, "You're quiet today, CJ. Something wrong?"

"No. What is there to say?"

"Whatever you want, baby. We used to be able to find a lot to talk to each other about."

"Not any more. I've said it all."

She drove on, silent, and David let her alone.

They topped a little ridge on the road, and just ahead, a pickup and car were parked. The pickup faced toward her, but the car was facing the other way behind the pickup, hiding it from her view.

David said, "There's Puna's pickup. Park in front of it."

There was just enough room on the shoulder left for her to pull in hood-to-hood with the pickup. Turnouts were few and far between on the narrow, unmarked road. Claudia turned off the engine and popped the trunk. The sun beat down hot on her, but she stayed in the car.

David got out and went to retrieve his camera equipment. "I could use a little help getting set up, CJ."

Claudia got out of the car to help him, wanting to do anything that would end this day sooner. David walked up and down the road, looking for a fairly level area in the lava to set his tripod on. He used his crutches to steady himself. Claudia knew without asking that he was wary of putting his full weight on the leg without having a way to support himself on the uneven terrain.

When David found a suitable place in the lava, he called to Claudia, "Bring the tripod and the black case up here."

Claudia climbed over the rough lava and thought she heard voices. She looked up through the brush and saw Puna's unmistakable form working his way down through the lava. Puna's brothers carried something between them on a pole, the dogs bounding along ahead of them.

David said, "Here they come. Go get the other bag for me while I get some shots of them coming down."

Claudia picked her way down to the car and glanced toward the car parked in back of the pickup. Since it was facing the same way her car was, she could see the driver's side window was rolled down. A man's shirt-sleeved arm rested on the car door. She went to the trunk to get the bag David wanted. As she came out from behind her car, she saw the man reflected in the car's outside mirror. His face was hidden by wraparound, mirrored sunglasses. She looked for the license plate, but the car was too close to Puna's pickup for her to see it. She crossed the road and carried the bag to David. He switched cameras on the tripod as Puna and his brothers closed the distance between them.

Claudia returned to her car and waited while David took pictures, positioning Puna and his brothers like a movie director. His crutches were at his side on the lava as he worked. He posed the men, who were carrying what Claudia could now see was a wild pig. After a few shots he had them lower the pig, remove it from the pole, and lift it onto Puna's shoulders, draping the dead animal around Puna's neck. David gestured for the dogs, and Puna called them and ordered them to sit at his feet as David took more pictures.

David kept taking pictures until he was satisfied he had gotten every angle and shadow just right. Then he let Puna and his brothers carry the pig to the back of the pickup. They returned to help David bring his equipment down off the lava, and David followed them to the back of the pickup. It was then that the man in the car opened his door and stepped out. He was a slight man with straight, black hair and an Oriental skin tone. He wore a white, long-sleeved shirt with the cuffs turned up. Sun glinted off a heavy looking gold watchband and a diamond ring on his finger. His black pants and black dress shoes looked expensive. He went between the vehicles and was out of sight. Claudia couldn't see what they were doing. Her view was effectively blocked by the pickup in front of her, but she heard them talking and then what sounded like a car trunk lid being closed. The man returned to his car with something in his hand that looked like an envelope. She heard the car engine start and saw the black, foreign-made sedan swing across the road and back up. The car window was closed now, and Claudia couldn't see the man at the wheel through the dark, tinted windows. After several attempts, the man got the car turned around and drove past Claudia. Without seeming to watch, Claudia noted the color and make of the car and memorized the license plate number.

She pretended to be uninterested in what was going on, but she had the sickening feeling David was involved in something more than just taking drugs. She was sure she had just witnessed a drug exchange, and she was angry with David for involving her if he was drug dealing. She had always suspected Puna of being into something illegal, but now it appeared David was involved, too. She was glad she would be leaving soon. The sooner the better, before something happened she would be implicated in.

Finally, David was done, and Puna helped carry David's bags to her car. The other two men corralled the dogs, got them into the back of the pickup, closed the tailgate, and climbed into the back of the pickup, too. They sat down against the cab of the truck, where Claudia couldn't see them. Puna got into the pickup and turned it around, heading back the same way he had come, from the Hana side of the mountain.

David settled into the passenger's seat. Claudia turned the small sports car around easily now that the turnout was empty, and they headed back along the road.

She wanted to say something to David about what he was doing, but knew it would do no good and only anger him. She really didn't want to know what he was involved in. Yet she understood now why he had tried to paint something different, something that would sell more easily than what he had been painting, and why he hadn't been painting at all. He had been making a living selling drugs—she was sure of it.

David finally said, "Will you be able to take me to the doctor next week, babe?"

"No, David. I've decided to go back to New York. I've got a flight out on Friday."

"When did this happen?"

"I just decided I needed to get back."

"Why?"

"I have a lot to do to get my orders taken care of."

He looked at her questioningly, but she avoided his eyes, keeping hers on the road. "This isn't like you, CJ. You never used to want to leave early. You always wished you could stay longer."

With resignation in her voice, she replied, "That was when I thought I'd found paradise. Now I know there is no such place."

"You still could have it all, baby—with me. I can give you everything you ever wanted. I can make paradise happen for you again. You know I can. I can love you better than any man alive. You know it's true. You've been there with me. Come back to me, CJ."

There was at least a kernel of truth in his words. And the longing to have again what they had once had together was almost overwhelming. But she knew that the paradise she had once experienced in his arms was gone—destroyed by another love: the love of drugs. "No, David. I'm going back to New York, and I'm not coming back."

"Then can I get you to do one last thing for me?"

"I don't know. What is it?"

"That suitcase I need to send to Rosa. It would get to her a lot faster if you just took it to her. I can give her a call and have her meet you at the LA airport. You'll be stopping there to change planes, right?"

"Yes, but I'm checking my luggage through."

"You can carry this on. It'll be no problem."

"I really don't want to do this, David. I'll take you to the post office so you can mail it."

"It'll take it a month to get there. She can't wait that long. She's got to have those papers and the pictures now, and her warm clothes."

With an edge to her voice, Claudia retorted, "If they were so important, why didn't you Fed Ex them already?"

"After we got back the other day, Puna called. Rosa remembered something else she needed. I had to wait until I saw Puna today to get it from him."

Claudia was mollified, but only a little. She didn't want any more to do with David, Puna, or his scatterbrained sister, Rosa.

"I can count on you to do it then?"

"No, David. I don't want to do this. This is Rosa's problem, not mine. Let her buy some warm clothes. And you can fax or e-mail the papers and pictures to her."

"That does not make a professional portfolio, and you know it. If you were an agent, would you accept a half-assed job like that?"

Claudia didn't answer.

"You told me I could depend on you, Claudia, and Rosa thought she could depend on you, too. She looks up to you. You gave her the encouragement to try this, and now you're letting her down when she needs your help the most."

There it was again—the guilt trip. Why did she always have to be Miss Goody Two-shoes? She had promised David she would help him, and now he was using her to help Rosa. She didn't even want to think about what David might have promised Rosa. Or what Rosa had provided David in return. She wasn't so naive as to think David hadn't taken the starstruck girl into his bed. It had been obvious to Claudia from the first time she met her that Rosa had been in love with David. Claudia made up her mind, but this was the last straw.

"All right, David. I'll take the suitcase to her, but this is it. This is the last thing I will do for you or any of your friends."

He laid his arm across the back of the seat and started rubbing the back of her neck.

She cried, "Stop it!" and tried to push his hand away, almost running off the road.

David grabbed the wheel with his other hand, and Claudia stepped on the brakes, bringing the car to a sudden, tire-screeching halt.

"My God, CJ! What's gotten into you?"

"You, David. You've used up all your favors. Now keep your hands off me."

The rest of the drive back to Lahaina was made in unyielding silence. She pulled in behind David's Jeep and stopped. She popped the lid on the trunk and got out to carry his camera bags into the studio. He was unlocking the door when she brought the first two bags to the entrance. He went in and held open the door for her, and she set the bags on the table. She returned to the car for more of David's equipment. He was opening a suitcase on the table. She set down the equipment and went back to the car. David was locking the suitcase when she brought in the last load.

"Okay. The suitcase is ready." He handed it off to her.

Without a word, she turned to leave.

"CJ, baby. You're not going to leave me like this, are you?"

She turned to look at him, sadness taking the place of anger in her—sadness for what once was and for what might have been. "I have to leave you like this, David. You give me no other choice."

"I'm sorry, baby. I didn't mean to hurt you. I love you."

"It's too late for that now. Good-bye, David, and good luck."

She went out the door and shut it. She was close to tears, but she fought them off with anger—anger at David, but even more anger at herself for letting herself be used.

She drove back to the hotel, pulled into the driveway, and let the attendant take her car. She climbed the steps to the veranda and steeled herself. She didn't want to see Chris, but she doubted she could avoid him. She looked straight ahead and kept walking, her sunglasses still on, ignoring everything.

"Claudia."

It was Chris. She stopped and faced him, cold and unyielding. His smile dimmed a little at her lack of response.

"I've been trying to call you. I still want to take you out to dinner. Would tonight be a good night?"

"Sorry, no. I have to pack."

A frown creased his forehead, "Pack? I don't understand."

"I'm leaving Friday."

"Oh? I thought you wanted to take a vacation."

"No. Please excuse me. I have things to do." She turned away from Chris but not before she saw the hurt in his eyes.

CHAPTER XI

Claudia called for the bellboy to come for her luggage and had her car brought to the lobby door. She was ready to leave. A feeling of despair and sadness swept over her, and she walked out to the veranda for one last look at the view of the gently waving palms and the dark, hulking mound of Lanai across the expanse of sparkling blue water. She'd had so many dreams here, and now they were all gone. She had been foolish enough to think she could make a life here without David, but now she knew she would never be free of him and the hold he had over her because she had loved him.

Then there was Chris, who had given her hope there could be someone after David, but not now. How could he ever respect her after the way she had acted? There was no way he could forget. It would always be there to taint their relationship. She had compromised the basis of their growing respect and friendship for each other by violating one of the principals she had been trying to instill in the girls she had chosen for the fashion show.

There was a knock on the door, and she turned away from the view she had ceased to see as tears of remorse welled in her eyes. She went to the door to open it for the bellboy.

With sunglasses covering her tearful eyes and her lips set in a grim line, she went to the desk to check out. Henri saw her and came out of his office.

"Claudia, *mon cher*! Are you leaving us?"

"Yes, Henri."

"But I thought you were staying longer! You haven't been down to discuss a date for next year. What has happened?"

"I'll have to get back to you, Henri. Something has come up, and I have to get back to New York. Please forgive me."

"Ah, mademoiselle, I am sorry. I will be looking forward to hearing from you. Please let me know if there is anything I can do to help."

"Thank you, Henri. You have been so kind. I appreciate all your help so very much, and I do thank you for everything. There is one thing you can do for me. I believe you have something in the security safe that belongs to me."

"Oh, yes, of course." He picked up the phone and punched in some numbers. She wanted to stop him. She didn't want to see Chris. She wanted to bolt out the door and leave the gun.

Henri was saying into the phone, "There is a case in the safe that belongs to Miss Jordan. Will you bring it to the front desk, please?"

She picked up her credit card and fumbled with her purse, rigidly focused on putting the card away. She heard footsteps coming across the teakwood floor and tensed even more.

"I believe this is yours, Miss Jordan."

Her eyes flew to his face. He smiled at her, but the smile did not reach his eyes. She saw only sadness there. She dropped her eyes to the gun and took it from him, saying, "Thank you." She walked stiffly toward the door, leaving Chris and Henri behind her.

At the airport, Claudia stood with her luggage in the agricultural inspection line, watching the inspectors with increasing frustration. Today of all days, the security equipment had failed, and a lone technician was studying the problem with Hawaiian lethargy. The agricultural inspectors were equally unhurried, their dark faces shining with sweat in the warmth of another sunny day in paradise. Damp patches of sweat darkened uniforms stretched tightly over ample Polynesian physiques as they methodically required every suitcase to be opened for inspection. Finally, it was Claudia's turn. She set her soft-sided suitcases on the table and opened them for inspection. The woman doing the inspection immediately saw the gun case in one suitcase and the separate shell case in the other.

"Do you have your papers for this weapon, ma'am?"

Claudia unzipped the inside pocket of her carry-on bag and handed the papers allowing her to transport the gun to the inspector. The woman looked at the papers without comment and handed them to the inspector who seemed to be in charge of the operation.

Claudia had noticed him earlier, going between the tables and overseeing the inspections. He was a Hawaiian of large proportions who looked like he took his job very seriously. Claudia was beginning to feel uncomfortable.

"Do you have a permit to carry this weapon, Miss Jordan?"

"Yes." She reached into her purse and handed the woman her driver's license and concealed-weapon permit. She stood with growing tension as the woman looked at the license and permit. She handed them back to her superior, who scrutinized them thoroughly.

After what seemed like an unusually long delay, the documents were all approved and returned to Claudia. She put everything away, trying to control the trembling anxiety she felt at the agonizing delay. She closed and locked her bags. The inspector labeled them, and she felt a moment of relief as she set her bags back onto the luggage cart.

"May we see the other bag, please?"

In the annoyance of having to clear her own bags, she had momentarily forgotten about Rosa's suitcase. She lifted it onto the table and flipped the latches, but the case was locked. Belatedly, she realized she didn't have a key to Rosa's suitcase.

"Do you have a key for this case?"

"No. I'm sorry, I don't have the key."

"Is this your suitcase?"

Claudia began to feel uncomfortable all over again. She sensed something ominous was happening and she was right in the middle of it. Her first instinct was to lie—to tell them she had lost the key. Then she remembered what her grandfather had told her when, as a child, she had tried to lie about snitching his candy: always tell the truth, and you won't have to worry about remembering what you said in a lie.

"No. I'm taking it to LA for a friend."

"Please come with us, Miss Jordan."

She could do nothing but comply. The chief inspector led her into an office while the woman inspector brought her luggage and set it in the office along with Rosa's suitcase.

The supervising inspector went around the desk and lowered his bulk into a chair that groaned a bit under the weight. "Please sit down, Miss Jordan. I need to ask you a few questions."

Claudia sat down.

"Do you know the person who gave you this suitcase?"

"Yes."

"The name, please?" It was an order, not a question.

"David Keanu."

"Do you know his address?"

"Yes." She gave the man David's address in Lahaina.

"Who were you taking the suitcase to?"

"A friend of his in LA."

"Do you have a name?"

"Her name is Rosa Halupa."

"Do you know her?"

"Yes." Claudia was getting more uncomfortable by the minute.

"What is her address?"

"All I know is she is in LA."

"How were you to get the suitcase to her?"

"She is meeting me at the airport."

"Do you know what is in the suitcase?"

"I was told it contains a portfolio with some papers and pictures she needs for modeling school and interviews. There is also a jacket and other clothes."

"Did you actually see those things in the suitcase?"

"No."

"Then you don't really know what the suitcase contains?"

"No." Claudia's palms were getting cold and clammy.

The inspector stood up. "I'm sorry, Miss Jordan, we will have to hold you until we can open the suitcase."

He hefted his bulk out of the chair and left her sitting in the room with his woman assistant standing behind her. Claudia sat still, her fingers clutching her purse in white-knuckled apprehension. All she could think of was how stupid she had been. She prayed there was nothing else in the suitcase, but her gut feeling told her there was, and David knew it. Everyone had known but her.

By the time the door opened again, Claudia was resigned to the fact she was in more trouble than she could handle. There was nothing she could say or do to prove she was innocent. She could deny nothing—not the fact she knew David, nor the fact she knew Rosa and Puna and had been to Wailua. And especially not the fact she had the suitcase. She couldn't even deny she knew David used drugs.

"Miss Jordan."

She turned to look at the person who spoke to her. The man wore a police uniform. A second policeman stood behind him in the doorway.

"Yes," she barely whispered.

"You'll have to come with us."

She was escorted, along with her luggage, to a police car, and driven away from the airport to the police station in Wailuku, the county seat of Maui. The police station was a newer, modern, concrete building located off Kaahumanu Avenue between Kahului and Wailuku.

The officer in the front seat picked up the radio and said into the mike, "We're comin' in the driveway. Open the door."

The car pulled around to the side of the building, and a huge double door opened into a concrete garage. The police car pulled to a stop. The door closed behind them before an officer opened the door to the backseat, where Claudia sat in troubled silence.

"You can get out of the car, Miss Jordan."

Claudia slowly exited the vehicle. The first officer was holding a door open in the corner of the garage. The officer with her took her arm and guided her toward the open door. She stepped inside and stopped, her face paling and her skin growing cold. She saw a cell at the end of the narrow room and a large window to the left. Several uniformed officers manning computers and other technical equipment turned their attention on her.

The officer with her said, "We need to fingerprint you, Miss Jordan. Please step up to the table."

His vicelike grip gave her no choice but to go with him.

She suffered through the fingerprinting and picture-taking process silently, cooperating, but feeling degraded and alone. After the formal booking process, the officers took her through to another office, where she saw a series of partitions filling the room on the left and a small cubicle of an office on the right. She was shown into the small cubicle. One of the officers stayed in the room with her; the other officer disappeared behind the partitions. Claudia seated herself behind the table to wait, afraid of what was to come. She knew she was going to be questioned as soon as they had time to find out what was in the suitcases. Waiting without explanation was part of the intimidation process. She resolved to remain calm and be truthful.

Finally, two men entered the room, followed by two uniformed officers. The first two men did not wear uniforms. One of them was Caucasian, the other Oriental. The Caucasian wore glasses and carried a tape recorder. The Oriental carried Rosa's suitcase, and he set it on top of the table. The latches were closed, but the lock had been punched out. They sat down in the chairs opposite Claudia.

"I'm Detective Cave, and this is Detective Omoto. Is this your suitcase, Miss Jordan?"

"No."

"But it is the suitcase you had with you at the airport?"

"Yes."

"For the record, Miss Jordan, would you tell us how you got the suitcase and why you had it in your possession?" He switched on the tape recorder.

Claudia paled and thought, *Why aren't they reading me my rights?* But she was afraid to ask it out loud. She answered, with her hands clenched tightly together in her lap, "A friend of mine asked me to deliver the suitcase to a friend of his in LA."

"Please state the name of the friend who gave you the suitcase."

"David Keanu."

"And who is the friend you were taking it to in LA?"

"Rosa Halupa."

"And how did Mr. Keanu get the suitcase?"

"We got it from Puna Halupa, Rosa's brother."

"Then you were with Mr. Keanu when he got the suitcase?"

"Yes. Mr. Keanu has a broken ankle and can't drive. I took him to get the suitcase."

"Where did you go to get the suitcase?"

"Wailua."

"Did you know what was in the suitcase?"

"I was told it contained a portfolio with some papers and pictures Miss Halupa needed, a jacket, and some warm clothes."

Detective Cave glanced at Detective Omoto. "Show Miss Jordan what is in the suitcase."

Detective Omoto unlatched the suitcase and opened it up to lay flat on the table. Claudia saw the portfolio, a jacket, a pair of sweatpants and a sweatshirt, and two ziplock bags of white powder. Detective Cave said, "Let the record show the suitcase has a portfolio, jacket, sweat suit, and two ziplock bags of powdered material."

Detective Cave held up one of the bags of white powder and asked, "Do you know what this is, Miss Jordan?"

"No."

"Please remember, Miss Jordan, that you are on tape. Do you wish to change your statement?"

Feeling frightened and uncertain, she answered with a tremor in her voice, "I don't know what it is, but I have an idea what it is, if that is what you are wanting me to say. And how do I know who put it in the suitcase? You could have put it there for all I know."

A brief smile touched Detective Cave's lips. Detective Omoto remained inscrutable. "Just answer the question, Miss Jordan."

She eyed the man, trying to decide how to answer. Everything was being recorded, and she wanted to make sure it was clear she did not know what the bags contained. "This is entrap—"

Before she got the word out, Detective Cave shut off the tape recorder. Claudia stopped speaking.

"Continue, please, Miss Jordan."

"I refuse to answer on the grounds it might incriminate me."

"You can't pull that crap here, Miss Jordan. This isn't a courtroom."

"And you haven't read me my rights, Detective Cave. I have a right to remain silent, and I have a right to an attorney to advise me."

Detective Cave looked at her with disgust. "Do you want to be charged with not cooperating, Miss Jordan?"

"I have been cooperating. I want to talk to a lawyer, please."

Detective Cave stood up and picked up the tape recorder. "You realize, Miss Jordan, that we already have enough evidence to convict you of drug dealing."

Claudia just looked at them, refusing to say another word until she had a lawyer.

The detectives left the room. The two policemen did not. Claudia resumed her wait. For what, she didn't know.

Another hour passed, and Claudia began to hurt from sitting so long in the wooden chair. She stood up, watching the two policemen who stood watch over her. They returned the scrutiny but said nothing. She began to move, walking back and forth in the few feet of space behind the table, but that brought on a more uncomfortable urgency.

She stopped before one of the policemen and said, "I need to use the restroom."

The other policeman opened the door and stepped out of the room. He came back shortly with a short, chunky, dark-skinned woman in a police uniform.

"Come with me, Miss Jordan."

Claudia followed the woman out of the room and into the corridor, the two uniformed officers trailing along behind. Claudia felt like a rat in a maze as she followed the policewoman through the angled corridor until they finally came to a door with a skirted figure on it. The policewoman pushed open the door and followed Claudia into the restroom. Claudia went into one of the stalls. The policewoman braced the door open with one arm and watched her. The questioning had been bad enough, but this was even more degrading.

Claudia came out of the stall, washed her hands, and turned, ready to leave. The policewoman opened the door for her and led her back through the corridor, the policemen following, until they were back in the office and inside the interrogation room. Claudia went around the table and stood with her hands gripping the chair back. She flexed her muscles from the bottom of her spine to her neck, and then paced the tiny cubicle until she could tolerate sitting again. She leaned back in the chair and closed her eyes, trying to forget everything that had happened to her.

The door opened. Claudia's eyes flew open at the sound, apprehension engulfing her. The two policemen left the room at some unseen bidding, and another man stepped into the room. Claudia's eyes widened with disbelief at the sight of Chris. Her whole body straightened with anticipation. Then she sank back, realization dawning on her. David had called Chris a cop, but Claudia had thought it was just a generalization David used when speaking of anyone doing any kind of work that involved law enforcement. David wasn't much different than Puna in his dislike for haoles and government. He had just learned to deal with it less aggressively.

Chris came around the table and sat down on the corner of it, one foot on the floor, one foot dangling between the table and the floor. He was so close to her he almost touched her. He was holding some papers in his hand. She saw a photo ID badge clipped to his shirt and a gold shield pinned to his shirt pocket.

Chris looked at her intently. With a gentle smile, he asked, "Are you okay, Claudia?"

"No. Are you here to question me, too?"

"No. The questioning is over for now."

"What does that mean? Are they going to charge me with something, or let me go?"

He laid the papers on the table in front of her. "You are being charged with possession and interstate transport of an illegal drug."

Claudia buried her face in her hands.

"Claudia," he said so softly it was a whisper. "I know you didn't know you had drugs in that suitcase. You got the suitcase from David, right?"

Claudia nodded her head, her face still covered with her hands, as tears welled in her eyes at having to betray David.

"I've arranged to have you released into my custody."

She raised her head and stared at him questioningly, wiping at the tears on her cheeks. "Why would you do that?"

He smiled. "It's either that or jail."

"I don't understand."

"I want to help you through this, but you've got to trust me, Claudia. I don't think you want jail time. I don't want you to endure that. Our jail isn't the Lahaina Gardens Hotel."

Claudia didn't have to think about it long. Jail was not an option she wanted to consider. She wished she could get beyond his soft voice and intimate smile to what he was really thinking and feeling. All the horror of the mugging and rape outside her New York office building came back to her in a flash. She couldn't blame Chris. She had trapped herself by believing in David. With Chris, she had been betrayed by her own body. There was really nothing she could do to prevent the events she had set in motion. She couldn't blame him for thinking the worst of her. So why was he doing this? She felt things were beyond her control no matter what she did now.

She shrugged and whispered resignedly, "All right."

Chris stood up and smiled at her. "Come on, Bonnie. I'm bustin' you out of this joint."

He picked up the papers and went to open the door. Claudia picked up her purse and rose to follow him. Chris stacked her luggage together, extended the handle, and motioned her through the door.

CHAPTER XII

Claudia felt a wave of relief when she was finally outside of the building. She stood beside Chris's four-wheel-drive vehicle while he put her luggage in the back. On the outside, the vehicle, a cross between a station wagon and the bigger sport-utility four-wheel drives popular on the mainland, looked a little worse for wear. The sun and salt water were taking a toll on the exterior. He opened the door for her, and she stepped up into the front seat. She realized then it was an unmarked police vehicle. There was a police radio attached under the dash. A portable red light rested in the passenger cup holder, and fastened against the driver's door was a scabbard holding a shotgun. The interior was in better condition than the exterior. Chris opened the driver's side door and got in beside her.

"Have you had anything to eat?"

"No."

"Good. This time you can't refuse to let me take you out to eat."

Chris started the rig, backed it out of the parking place, and turned it toward the driveway leading out of the police parking lot onto Kanaloa Avenue. He drove to a café close to the police station and took her inside. A waitress brought them water and menus. Chris didn't have to look at the menu to know what he wanted.

Their order came, and they ate in strained silence. He paid the bill, and they were soon back in his vehicle and going up Kaahumanu Avenue, headed for the junction with Honoapiilani Highway. Claudia was silent, looking out the window on her side of the vehicle.

"Are you going to be able to handle being in my custody?"

She shook her head. "I don't know. I thought I knew who you were, but now everything I thought I knew is false."

"No, everything I told you is true. I just couldn't tell you everything. I wanted to, but then I found out you were David Keanu's friend."

"What does David have to do with you?"

"He's a suspected drug dealer. The department's been watching him for months. We've been trying to get enough evidence to pick him up. I couldn't let you know I was watching him."

Claudia felt betrayed. Her voice revealed her surprise and pain. "You were using me to keep track of David?"

"What would you have done in my place? I have a job to do, and I use any resources I can to get the job done. I'm sorry you got caught in the middle of it. Believe me, Claudia. I would change things if I could."

Claudia turned her head away from him and didn't say any more. Her thoughts were a whirlpool of doubts. She wondered what Chris's purpose was with her now. Why should he care what happened to her? She had provided him with the evidence he needed to charge David. She would have been better off in jail.

"Claudia, I told you you'd have to trust me. I didn't want to have to use you, but I didn't have a choice. In using you to shut down this drug operation, I can clear you of the charges against you. I will testify you willingly worked with me."

"How long do you think this will take?"

"I can't answer that, but I think things will come to a head quickly now that we have your testimony."

"And what about David?"

"He'll be arrested. So will Puna and Rosa."

"There was another man."

"Who?"

"I don't know. The day I took David out to do a photo shoot on the back side of Haleakala. He met Puna and Puna's brothers. There was another man waiting there in a car. I got his license number."

Chris gave Claudia glorious smile. "Wonderful! Did you get a look at him? Could you identify him in a lineup?"

"No. All I can tell you is that he looked Asian. He had black hair, and his pants and shoes looked expensive—as in designer expensive. He was wearing a big, flashy diamond ring and a watchband that looked like it was solid gold. He was wearing mirrored sunglasses. I really couldn't see all of his face. When he turned his car around, he was headed west. He had rolled up his window and the glass was tinted, so it was impossible to see him. That's when I got his license number."

"Did you see any drugs?"

"No, but I'm sure something was going on. I stayed in the car. I didn't want to know what they were doing. I didn't want to be involved. I didn't want to take the suitcase to Rosa. That's why I was leaving to go back to New York. I didn't want to have to deal with David anymore."

Claudia felt the tears welling up in her eyes and constricting her throat. She turned her head away and looked out the window at the view of the West Maui Mountains. Subdivisions and golf courses had been built on the gentle lower slopes where there had once been fields of sugarcane.

"Give me that license plate number. I want to start a check on it before the DMV closes."

"ODQ 734."

Chris lifted the mike off the radio under the dash, turned up the volume knob, and pushed the send button on the mike.

"Officer Hadley, 15007, calling Wailuku."

Almost immediately, there was an answer. "Go ahead, Hadley."

"Need an ID on Hawaii license plate ODQ 734."

"Roger, ODQ 734."

"Roger, out."

In a few more miles they rounded the Papawai Point. Chris said, "There's a cell phone in the compartment in front of you. Would you get it out for me?"

Claudia opened the compartment and retrieved the phone, holding it out to Chris.

"Check the battery. If it's okay, I want you to call a number for me."

"The battery's okay."

"Call 699-4900."

Claudia punched in the numbers, waited until she heard the first ring, and handed the phone to Chris. "It's ringing."

"Hi. This is Chris Hadley. Is Henri in the office?"

Claudia looked at him questioningly.

"Henri, this is Chris. I need a room with twin beds. Do you have anything available for the next several days?"

A frown crossed Chris's face as he listened to the response on the other end. "Okay, Henri. I'll need to get into it as soon as I can in the morning. Mahalo."

He handed the phone back to Claudia. "Henri doesn't have a room available until tomorrow."

"What does that mean?"

He glanced at her with a half smile. "That means you'll have to spend the night at my place."

Claudia looked at him, wondering what difference it made. Anywhere would be better than jail.

The light on his police radio started flashing. He picked up the mike and turned up the volume. He pushed the button on the mike and said, "Columbus here."

A voice came back over the speaker. "You on your way in, CC?"

"Roger."

"Are you having company for dinner?"

"Roger. You got your fish yet?"

"Negative. Just got the fishing license. I'll be in touch tomorrow."

"Add a John Doe to that license."

"Roger. Out."

Chris hung the mike back on the radio and turned the volume down. "That was one of the men I work with."

They entered Lahaina. Chris stayed on the highway until they got to Kenui Street and turned toward Front Street, driving past the Lahaina Gardens Hotel. Claudia wasn't sure where he was going when he turned on Front Street and stopped to make a left turn onto Ala Moana. There were only a couple of houses on this street. Beyond them was the

Jodo Mission. Across the street from the mission was an old cemetery. But Chris didn't turn down Ala Moana Street. He angled off onto a street leading to Mala Wharf. He pulled his vehicle into the large, fenced area to the right of the road and parked.

A feeling of apprehension crawled up Claudia's spine. "Where exactly do you live?"

He turned to look at her. "Remember when I asked if you would like to go sailing?"

"Oh, no! You don't live on a boat, do you?"

He nodded.

"But why?"

"A matter of economics. It's a long story. Do you want to hear about it now or wait until we're on the boat?"

"Now would be better." Anything to delay having to go on a boat!

"Maui County is short of money, and the Hawaii state government is out of money. We're running out of money to operate essential services like the police department. The Lahaina department was going to have to cut its payroll. That meant men with less seniority than me were going to be laid off. One of the men, a good young officer who happens to be a friend of mine, is buying a home and has two little kids. I didn't want to see him lose his job, so I made a deal with the department to try to save his job.

"A couple of years ago, I had the chance to buy this sailboat really cheap from a guy who was going back to the mainland for good. He'd been living on the boat and working in Lahaina, but he finally decided he was tired of it. He wanted quick cash, so I got a good deal and fulfilled one of my lifelong dreams of owning a sailboat.

"I already knew Henri from the trouble I told you about. Henri wanted a security system installed. I told him I'd put it in for him if he would hire me as his security man. I let my apartment go and moved onto the boat so I could live on the salary Henri could pay me. From my office in the hotel, I do computer work for the police department in exchange for keeping my medical and pension plan in effect. And the department was able to keep a darn good man."

Claudia looked at him, finally understanding. There was no duplicity here—just a man who had given up his salary so another man could keep his.

"That was him on the radio, wasn't it?"

"Who?"

"The man you gave up your job for."

"How do you know that?"

"The way you looked when you heard his voice."

"And how was that?"

"It was the kind of look a person gets when they care about someone."

He laughed. "Well, I guess I do care about Mark. They assigned him to me the first day he came on the force. We've been together ever since."

"Then the feeling must be mutual."

"Yeah, I guess it is. Well, let's see what kind of a sailor you are."

"You don't want to know."

He grinned at her. "I'll take my chances."

Reluctantly, Claudia got out of the four-by-four. Chris was already out of the vehicle and unloading her luggage. "You got some deck shoes in here?" he asked.

"I think I can find my tennies."

Claudia unzipped the larger bag and had to dig clear to the bottom to find the canvas shoes she had brought. She took off her heels and slipped the rubber-soled canvas shoes onto her stockinged feet. When she had her shoes stowed and the bag zipped, Chris took charge of her luggage, and she followed him toward the crumbling concrete structure that had been Mala Wharf. Anchored to the riprap of boulders that kept the ocean from washing away the rest of the battered old pier were several small boats.

"Stay here. I'll get the boat up closer to the ramp so you won't have to try to balance on the rocks."

He slipped off his deck shoes and socks. Now she understood why he wore the canvas slip-ons. He rolled up his cotton twill pants and slipped the rubber-soled shoes on his feet. With practiced skill, Chris stepped from one sea-washed boulder to the next until he got to a small rubber boat. Its motor looked like a toy canted over a mounting bracket at the back of the raft. With one pull on the starter rope, the engine choked to life. In a few minutes he had nosed the rubber craft into the paved ramp at her feet. He set her bags inside the raft and offered her his hand.

Very carefully, Claudia stepped into the craft. It felt like she was stepping into Jell-O. She turned uncertain eyes to him, and he reassured her.

"It's okay. Just sit down on the front. I'll try not to get you wet."

Chris waded into the water, pushing the raft along the ramp until it was clear of the rocks. He stepped into the back of the craft, gave the motor a pull, and spun it around by the control arm to pull the raft backward, away from the rocks. Then he turned the raft around by slowly returning the handle to the front position. Claudia hung on to the rope threaded through rubber eyelets on the boat with white knuckles. They rolled gently over the small swells rolling into the shore.

Several minutes later, Chris nosed the little raft into the back of a black-hulled, single-masted sailboat, one of several anchored just offshore. Deftly, he tied the raft to brackets mounted on either side of a portable boarding ladder hooked over the narrow transom of the boat. Chris took her luggage out first. He set it on the deck and extended his hand to Claudia, who was still holding the rope on the rubber raft in a death grip.

He grinned down at her, still offering her his hand. "I thought you celebrities spent all your time sailing up and down the Hudson River and around Long Island."

"I'm not one of them."

She took his hand, and he helped her onto the boat. He gestured toward the door next to the wheel of the sailboat. "Come down into the cabin and you can change into something more comfortable. You might as well relax and enjoy the view. Sunset is in another hour. If you're not too picky, I can fix us some supper."

"I don't think I should eat anything."

"I fix a mean fish of the day."

"What kind of fish?"

"Whatever I can catch."

"You catch it. I'll decide after you cook it whether I want any."

"You got yourself a deal, Miss Jordan."

He went down the steps into the cabin with her bags and held up his hand to help her down. "Watch your head."

She ducked just in time to avoid cracking her head against the low doorframe. Small windows down each side of the cabin structure let in light. To the left was a small galley; to the right, a table that could squeeze four around it.

"The head is behind the door on the right, forward from the table. Keep going forward and you'll find the bunks."

Claudia kept going, ducking to avoid another doorway that could be closed to separate the head and sleeping area from the galley. She passed into the sleeping quarters. Just inside the doorway on both sides were long, covered cushions that would sleep one person against each side of the hull. Into the forward-narrowing curve of the hull was a larger cushioned area that could sleep two people. A double sleeping bag and pillows covered that area. It made Claudia wonder how many overnight guests he had invited aboard to share the double sleeping bag. The thought had no more than passed through her mind before she felt ashamed for having judged him when she had no right to.

Chris set her bags on one of the single cushions and said, "Make yourself at home. I'll change out here." He pulled open a drawer under one of the bunks and retrieved a pair of shorts. "I'll be up catching dinner if you need me."

He slid the pocket door closed, and she was alone in the dusky light of the cramped sleeping quarters. She was already beginning to feel queasy at the gentle rise and fall of the boat as the swells lifted it on their way to the shore. Claudia opened a suitcase and pulled out slacks and a T-shirt. She might as well get as comfortable as she could, especially if she was going to have to sleep in her clothes. She folded her dress and pantyhose, put them into the suitcase, and zipped it closed again. She dug in her purse for her Dramamine and swallowed the pills without water.

She could hear Chris on the deck. She slid open the door between the galley and sleeping area and climbed the steps to the open air. The sun was sinking lower over Lanai, turning the few puffy clouds crowning the island crest into a soft shade of rosy gold. Chris was forward on the deck, casting into the gently lapping waters of the ocean, which turned a deeper blue as the sun slipped ever lower in the sky.

"You can come up here if you want. Just hang on and keep your feet on the rubber steps."

Claudia climbed up to the narrow catwalk skirting the cabin and, holding on to the handrail, cautiously moved forward along the narrow walkway until she was able to step out onto the broader forward deck. She sat down, taking in the view of the shoreline but preferring to look at the sunset and Chris, casting his line into the water. Suddenly, he jerked on the line and started reeling it in.

Claudia eyes followed the line into the water, asking, "Did you get something?"

"Yeah. I'll have him aboard in a minute."

She watched the taut line and saw a swirl and a flash of fin. Chris kept the line taut, slowly reeling in his resisting catch. When he got the fish up to the boat, he deftly walked along the cabin, dropped down into the back of the boat, and reached for the net hanging against the side of the boat. Claudia followed cautiously, not wanting to miss anything.

"Here," he said, handing her the pole. "Keep your hand on the reel and don't let the tip down."

Claudia protested. "But what if I lose it?"

"Then we'll just have to catch another one."

She took the pole, and he made sure she was holding it upright before he bent over the side of the boat with the net. The fish made a run, and the reel stripped line. Claudia gasped, "I don't know if I can hold him."

"Just don't let go of the reel and keep the line tight. When you feel it start to slack off, start reeling."

Memories of her childhood flashed through her mind. She was fishing in the creek behind grandfather's farm. It had been so long ago she had almost forgotten about it, but now Chris's voice brought up the long-forgotten experience. She remembered her grandfather saying almost the same thing to her. Her hands, long out of practice, remembered the feel of the line, the tension of the pole, and the steady grip on the reel. As soon as she felt the fish begin to tire, she started reeling in, keeping the line taut and the pole tip high.

Chris was bent over the side of the boat, holding the net. He looked back at her and grinned, saying, "Good! Good!"

The fish was turned toward the boat once more. Claudia didn't allow it to run again, bringing it slowly and surely to the net Chris had submerged in the water. With the skill of a born fisherman, Claudia guided the fish into the net, and Chris scooped the fish out of the water. He looked at her with a grin that made her heart skip a beat.

"You've done this before."

"Not in an ocean. My grandfather tried to teach me to fish in the creek on his farm in Iowa, but I didn't like threading worms on hooks."

"If you want to fish, I'll be glad to bait your hook for you."

"No. It's not a priority anymore."

Chris was down on the deck, removing the hook from the fish. When he had it free, he held the line up and Claudia reeled it in until she could catch the hook on an eye of the pole. "Just lay it on top of the cabin. I'll get it later. Right now I need to fillet this fish for supper. Down in the galley, there's a drawer to the right of the sink. Would you bring me the long, slender knife?"

Claudia stepped down into the darkening cabin. She found the knife and brought it up to Chris. The sun was gone, and only deepening shades of red and violet crowned the crest of Lanai across the water. A spout of water erupted from the darkening cobalt blue of the ocean a few hundred yards out from the boat, and a long, black shadow of a fin curved out of the water. Then the larger black fork of a tail lifted out of the water for a long moment before it disappeared into the blue depths. She couldn't see beyond this moment, but for this space in time she felt a tranquility she hadn't felt in days.

Claudia stayed on deck while Chris fixed supper. The fish smelled good enough to eat, and she was getting hungry. Up here on the deck, watching the shoreline with the twinkling lights of Lahaina reflecting in the water and the moon rising with a golden glow behind the West Maui Mountains, she relaxed. She felt a returning sense of something worth trying for, something worth hanging on to.

Chris called, "Supper's ready. You want me to bring it up there?"

"Yes. It's beautiful up here."

Chris, lithe and surefooted, came up the stairs with a plate in each hand. He handed Claudia a plate and asked, "Want coffee?"

"Sure."

He was back in a minute with steaming cups of coffee.

Claudia was savoring her first bite of the fish they had caught. "This is wonderful. How did you fix this?"

"A little olive oil, garlic, herbs, and wine. But don't praise me too much. I'm just a one-dish wonder."

As the sky darkened with the setting of the sun, Chris had to light a lantern so they could see to finish their supper. A breeze began to blow. Claudia felt the cooler air and rubbed her arms.

"Want to come below?"

"No. It's beautiful out here. I'd like to stay a while longer."

"I'll get you a sweatshirt."

He turned off the battery-operated lantern and gathered up the dishes to take them below. In a couple of minutes, he was back with a sweatshirt for her. Then he disappeared below again. She pulled the shirt over her head. The fragrance he wore mingled with the odor of his body lingered in the shirt. She breathed deeply of it, feeling her senses reacting to it and a flush of warmth sweep through her. She fought the feeling down. She couldn't let that happen again. She didn't need the pain and anguish of another failed relationship. She was finally feeling comfortable with Chris, and she didn't want to ruin whatever respect he still might feel for her.

After a while, Chris came on deck again. He stood looking at the sky and stars that appeared so much brighter away from the landmass and artificial lights. A few clouds came off the top of Lanai and were drifting toward the West Maui Mountains in the gentle breeze. The ocean was calm, the small swells whispering softly against the hull of the boat as they surged incessantly toward the shore.

Lights appeared on the reef a few hundred yards away. Claudia saw them and asked, "What are they doing with those lights out there?"

"Some of the locals are night fishing."

"What do they catch at night they can't catch during the day?"

"There are a number of things that are more active at night, like squid."

"I think you are about to ruin my supper."

"You asked."

Claudia was silent for a moment, leaning back with her elbows on the cabin roof and looking up at the stars. "That question you asked Mark. It was about David, wasn't it?"

"You're scaring me, Miss Jordan. Are you some kind of psychic?"

"No. Just able to put two and two together."

"They have the warrants ready for David, Puna, and Rosa."

"What's going to happen to David?"

"He'll probably get prison time." He seemed to mull something over. "How did you meet him?"

Claudia had caught the edge in Chris's voice and sensed his hesitation. She could feel his anxiety, and she realized the question he asked was not the question he wanted an answer to. She wondered how she could possibly explain David to Chris. She only knew that he had attracted her like no other man had been able to. In retrospect, she was sure it had been physical attraction and admiration for his art. Then, after reading about the history and culture of the Hawaiian people, she had romanticized about David, imagining him as one with the paintings he had created, until she felt she knew him—loved him. She had built a fantasy around him because of his paintings and the bygone culture he captured in them. It had taken a long time to finally become disillusioned. Now that she was removed from the stress she had been under, it was difficult to feel angry with David. She was even beginning to feel guilty for not lying for him.

She said, "We met on Kaanapali Beach the first time I came to Hawaii to do a photo shoot. He was there, painting." She was overwhelmed with the memory and had to look away. Then she asked, "Would it be possible to send him to a drug treatment program?"

"It might be. It would be your decision. You're the one who will have to testify for or against him."

"I don't want to destroy him. I just want him to quit the drugs and alcohol. He's a wonderful artist, but now there are too many artists here for him to compete with and still make a living. I saw the latest painting he did. He is trying to paint whales. That is not what inspires him. I think that is why he went into drugs. He needed the money.

"When I first met him, I don't believe he was into the hard drugs. He was using marijuana for pain. He told me he'd been hit by a car when he was riding his bicycle down Haleakala." Claudia paused. She couldn't tell Chris what it was like being with David. It wouldn't be fair to Chris. "He didn't drink to excess then, but the drinking got worse, and so did the drugs. That's when I decided I couldn't stay with him anymore."

Chris nodded. "I know about the accident. A local artist nearly killed by a hit-and-run driver. I was one of the investigators." He straightened up and said, "We can talk to the judge about doing something for him. A judge will usually consider alternatives if it's a first-time offense."

Claudia felt cold. David's future was in her hands. She had to do what she could to save him.

"You want to go below now? I've got some coffee left."

She unfolded her legs and stood up. "I suppose so. It's been a long day."

Chris led the way down the steps and into the cabin. Claudia followed.

"Where do you want me to bunk?" Claudia asked

"Wherever you want. This table turns into a bed and will give you more room than the single cushions forward. You can have one of my sleeping bags and a pillow, but I can't promise you clean sheets."

She took the coffee he held out to her and slid behind the table, getting a closed-in feeling in the cramped cabin. "How about on the deck?"

"You might get wet by morning."

"Well, I guess this will work."

They finished their coffee and Chris made the table into a bed for her. "You want to use the head first?"

"Sure. Just let me get my toothbrush." She retrieved her small bag from the forward cabin and opened the head door. There was no place in the tiny compartment to put her bag. She brought it into the galley and opened it, finding her toothbrush. She closed herself into the head and decided it was smaller than an airplane restroom. Fear of small places wasn't her problem, fortunately, but before she had her teeth brushed, she felt the beginnings of uneasiness in her stomach.

She came out of the head and back into the galley. Chris had a sleeping bag and pillow on the bed. She sat down to take off her canvas shoes. It was too warm to get inside the sleeping bag, so she lay on top of it, tucking her feet inside the bottom end of it. She punched up the pillow for her head. The subtle, male scent of Chris enveloped her again.

He came down the steps from the deck and said, "I'll leave the doors open. Just call me if you need anything." He turned off the light in the galley and went into the head.

◆   ◆   ◆

Claudia awoke in the night. The boat was rocking, and her stomach was pitching threateningly. She got up and felt for the ceiling light, feeling sick. She found the switch and, not a moment too soon, got into the head before she threw up.

Chris's voice penetrated her retching. "Oh, my God, Claudia! You weren't kidding about getting seasick. Come on. Let's get you up on deck."

He pulled her to her feet and got her up on deck before she had to throw up again. She leaned over the rail and stayed in that position.

"Don't keep your head down. Stand up and look toward the shoreline. It will help you get your equilibrium back."

She pushed herself upright, but as soon as she did, she had to throw up again. She doubled over the rail once more. When she was through, Chris pulled her upright, and she sagged against him. He put his arms around her and held her, her head against his shoulder. She felt another spasm coming, and he released her until she was finished. She was too weak to stand. Her knees wobbled, and she began to sink toward the deck. Chris grabbed her and kept her from falling. He lowered her to the deck. She leaned weakly against the hull, her eyes closed. A cold sweat beaded her face.

Chris left her and came back with a wet hand towel. Gently, he wiped her face, blotting the coolness against her lips.

Claudia opened her eyes and whispered, "I'm sorry, Chris."

He smiled a little crookedly at her. "You tried to warn me. Do you feel up to trying to go back to bed?"

She shook her head weakly. "I think I'd better stay right here."

"This isn't the best place, either. Come on down into the cabin and we'll go up on the front deck through the front hatch."

He helped her to her feet and held on to her as she negotiated the stairs, staggering like a drunk. He picked up the sleeping bag she was using, went through the forward cabin, and pulled down the ladder hooked to the ceiling. He stepped up on the ladder and unlatched the forward hatch. A breeze immediately swept through the cabin. He held out his hand to Claudia and pulled her up the ladder behind him. He wrapped the sleeping bag around her, turning her so her back was to him. He sat down with his back against the mast and eased her down to sit in front of him, between his legs.

She leaned her head against his shoulder and sighed, "This is much better."

Chris murmured in agreement. Finally, Claudia slept.

An hour before dawn, Claudia was awakened by the rain on her face. She noticed the boat was rocking more severely. The wind was more than a gentle breeze, and a Maui mist was falling. She turned in Chris's arms and said, "Wake up. It's raining!"

Chris awoke with a start and swiped at the rain on his face. "We'd better get below before we get soaked."

Claudia crawled away from him toward the hatch, trailing the sleeping bag. Chris followed, backing down the ladder after her. He found the lantern switch, and soft light illuminated the cabin. Claudia was sitting on one of the side bunks near the door, the sleeping bag wrapped around her. She was beginning to feel sick again. He closed the hatch and raised the ladder back up to fasten against the ceiling.

"I think I'd better take you back to shore. Think you can stand a little boat ride?"

She nodded grimly.

"Okay. I've got to throw a few things into a bag."

Claudia stood up and took the sleeping bag into the galley. She set the table and cushions back up and spread the sleeping bag over the tabletop to dry. She went into the head and washed her face and hands, the taste of seasickness still in her mouth. She tried to brush her teeth, but that only made her gag. She rinsed her mouth with mouthwash and let it go at that. Her face, in the tiny mirror above the miniature stainless-steel sink, was hollow-eyed and strained. She opened the door and stepped out into the narrow passage. Chris was already on deck.

He called down to her. "Are you ready?"

"As ready as I'll ever be."

Chris helped her into the rubber boat. It was bouncing like a carnival ride. "Get down on the bottom. I don't want you going swimming."

Claudia crawled forward on hands and knees and sat on the rain-soaked bottom of the boat. Chris loaded her luggage and his bag and stepped down into the little rubber craft. He got the motor started before he untied the ropes anchoring them to the back of the sailboat. In moments, they were bouncing over the choppy water toward the shoreline a few hundred yards away.

In spite of her apprehension, they made the boat ramp. Claudia, glad to be on shore again, scrambled out of the raft, soaking her feet in the process. She held on to the rope ringing the craft. She was already soaked through from the wind-driven rain, but it wasn't cold and it helped revive her.

Chris hauled the little rubber boat out of the water and up on the ramp. "I'll moor it when it's light out." He handed Claudia her purse, took their bags, and headed for the gate into the fenced area where his vehicle was parked. In another few minutes they were out of the rain and wind.

"Better find something dry to put on before anyone else shows up."

Chris was already stripping out of his wet shirt in the front seat. There was just enough light from the security light near the gate to allow Claudia to identify clothes in her suitcase as she leaned over the back of the seat. By the time she had somehow gotten into dry clothes and wrapped her big, warm, terrycloth robe around her, it was beginning to get light.

"I'm going out to secure the rubber boat. I'll be back in a little while."

Claudia looked after him as he ran through the wind-whipped rain toward the rubber raft on the ramp. Headlights turned down the road to the ramp and picked up Chris as he dragged the raft back into the water. The pickup stopped by the gate. Claudia sank down onto the seat and curled up, thoroughly exhausted, she fell asleep.

Claudia woke up when Chris opened the door to the vehicle just as the cell phone rang.

Chris answered the phone. "Yes?"

Claudia sat up.

Chris said, "Thanks. We'll be there in a few minutes."

"Is everything all right?" Claudia asked.

Chris turned his head and gave her a smile. "Yes. That was Henri. Our room is ready at the hotel."

Claudia smiled back. "Thank heaven."

CHAPTER XIII

It wasn't the suite on the fourth floor, but it was a big improvement over Chris's cramped sailboat. Claudia let Chris use the bathroom first. From the backseat she had seen the gooseflesh on his bare arms as he drove her to the hotel. He was dressed only in wet shorts and his boat shoes. She at least was drier than he was and keeping warm in her robe.

He came out of the bathroom and said, "All yours."

She picked up the things she had set out to take into the bathroom and luxuriated in a hot bath and being able to wash her hair. She put on clean, dry clothes. When she came out of the bathroom an hour later, she felt like herself again.

Chris was on the veranda, talking on the cell phone. She joined him. She leaned against the railing, looking out at the ocean. It was sunlit and blue now that the little rain shower had passed.

"Claudia." The tone of his voice made her turn to look at him. His face was devoid of expression, and his eyes were hooded.

"What is it?"

"That was Mark on the phone. They went to pick up David this morning. They found him dead."

Claudia looked at him for a moment, the words not registering. Then it hit her like a blow to the stomach. She whispered, "Oh, no!" But she knew it was true. She had never seen Chris look as he did now. Every muscle in his face was tense with what he was feeling. His eyes had turned to flint. Claudia put her hands to her face and sobbed.

Chris rose from his chair and took her in his arms. She swayed against Chris, weak and trembling with grief, her sobs shaking her to her very core. She still loved David. In spite of what the drugs had done to him, she had never wanted him dead.

Finally, Claudia could cry no more. She was empty of tears and empty of emotion. She was still shaking, and she clung to Chris, finding comfort in his silent compassion, feeling it in the touch of his hand on her hair. With an effort, she straightened in his arms and said, "I'll be all right now."

"Are you sure?" His eyes were no longer hard and cold. They gazed at her with sympathy and something that she didn't want to put a name to.

She nodded. "Do you know what happened?"

"Mark said it looked like a drug overdose."

Claudia sat down in one of the chairs on the veranda, engulfed in sadness. She felt guilty for not having been able to stop David from destroying himself.

"Mark wanted me to come over. Will it be all right with you if I go?"

She nodded, feeling numb.

"Do you want me to order you something to eat before I leave?"

She shook her head. "No. I don't feel like eating right now."

"I'll bring something up for us when I come back. Do you have your gun on you?"

She looked up at him questioningly. "No."

"Get it and keep it on you. Don't let anyone in but me. I want you to stay inside the room. Keep the veranda doors locked and the drapes and window louvers closed so that no one can see you."

Her face paled. "What are you telling me?"

"That you could be in danger. I'll know more after I talk to the people at David's. I don't want to take any chances that this was not an accidental death. You saw someone and got a license plate number. That person won't want to leave witnesses if he thinks you can ID him."

She nodded. He gave her a wan smile and reached out to touch her hair reassuringly before he left. She heard the door shut. More tears welled up to blur her vision as she moved inside and closed the veranda doors, drew the drapes, and closed the louvered shutters on the screened openings beside each door.

♦ ♦ ♦

Chris walked the few blocks to David's studio. There was no use driving. Lahaina Town didn't have enough parking for all the tourists as it was. The streets were already crowded with them, and the cruise ship in the harbor had deposited several hundred more tourists onto the narrow sidewalks. But he had to think of it as helping the community's economy, even though it was hell on the narrow streets and caused major traffic jams on the highway into and out of the quaint old whaling town.

Police cars were parked in front of the studio and the sidewalk cordoned off with yellow police tape. Two policemen stood guard. There were already a few curious onlookers across the street, trying to see what was going on. Chris hated that trait in people, wondering what they found so interesting at accident and murder scenes. He hadn't wanted to tell Claudia about Mark's suspicions, but Mark had good instincts. He thought Keanu had been murdered. Chris's gut feeling agreed with him.

One of the policemen standing guard in the street gave Chris a nod and let him come through the line. "Good morning, Sergeant Hadley."

"Good morning, Moko. Is Detective Mitsuro inside?"

"Yes, sir."

Chris ducked under the tape and said, "Mahalo."

Chris approached the front door of the studio and stopped as he saw the paintings showcased in the windows on either side of the door. He changed direction and stood outside the window to the right of the door, staring at the large painting displayed on an easel.

This was the painting Claudia had mentioned. She hadn't thought it was David's best work, but Chris thought it was very good. It was at least as good as some of the artists who specialized in whale paintings. A female whale was in the crystal blue water off Lahaina. Her head and one fin was out of the water, one eye on her baby, concern apparent in her look. Her newborn calf, still dangling the umbilical cord, was in the air above the water, its fins barely extended. It looked helpless and lifeless, suspended between life and death, between the world of light and air, a paradise of golden beaches and gently swaying palm trees, and the dark, forbidding depths of the sea, where the baby would perish if it couldn't breathe. There was a poignancy in the work that reached out to Chris. It obviously hadn't reached Claudia, but he saw what she hadn't seen: David's cry for help. He pulled his eyes away and went to the other window, where several of David's other paintings were clustered. The scenes were exquisitely done by a man who felt deeply about his heritage. The paintings were a blend of contemporary Hawaii and the Hawaii of the old Hawaiians, before white men and their missionaries came. Chris looked at each one, admiring the work.

The first painting was of a fisherman sitting in a folding chair along the beach south of Lahaina. There was foam cooler with a can of beer on top beside the chair. A heavy, barrel-chested Hawaiian man sprawled in the chair holding a pole, his economy-sized pickup parked in the trees along the beach behind him, the West Maui Mountains in the background. Beside the twentieth-century fisherman, a group of muscular Hawaiian men in loincloths from an earlier century were launching their outrigger canoe, hollowed from a log, into the gentle surf. They carried handmade nets, gourd floats, and hand-sharpened wooden spears.

Another painting showed the modern method of night fishing on the reefs with flashlights, lanterns, and spear guns. Beside the T-shirted, twentieth-century men in cutoffs stood ancient Hawaiian men. Their wooden torches cast an eerie glow on the water as they stood poised with their long, slender wooden spears. A third painting showed a young woman, looking very much like the girl Nani Li'i, working in her family's taro patch, her jeans rolled to the knees as she waded through the nodding green leaves with her plastic bucket, gathering roots. Ahead of her the ancient ones waded with their tapa-cloth skirts tucked up around their waists, their breasts covered only by their long black hair, carrying baskets hand woven from palm fronds. The fourth painting in the window pictured a Hawaiian father showing his young son the petroglyphs carved into the stone cliffs at Olowalu. The boy's finger was tracing one of the carved figures. On the buttress of stone next to the young father, a white-haired old man stood, diligently chipping away at the rock with stone tools, the beginnings of a figure discernable in the stone. Seated on the ground behind the old man, a younger man was sharpening stone chisels. A child stood with a hand on his shoulder, gazing up at the old man in quiet reverence.

Chris turned toward the door of the studio with a better understanding of and a new respect for the man he had only felt contempt for in life. He tapped on the front door of the studio and waited. He didn't want to touch anything without knowing if the detectives had dusted everything for prints. He saw Mark coming to let him in and smiled at his friend. Mark was a few years younger and quite a few inches shorter than Chris. He was island-born of a Japanese family. His great-great-grandparents had come to the islands in the 1800s.

"How you doing this morning, Detective Sergeant Hadley?"

Chris grinned at Mark's question, knowing it was really two questions. He hadn't been able to hide his interest in Claudia from his wiry, black-haired, brown-eyed friend. Unfortunately, Mark had a double-edged sense of humor, and he could read Chris like a book. "None of your damn business, Detective Mitsuro."

"Uh-oh. She must not have liked microwaved fish."

"She loved my fish. She thought it was better going down though than coming up."

Mark laughed, his almond eyes squinting almost shut with mischievousness. "So that's what I smell. I thought maybe you were trying a new perfume."

Because of his feelings for Claudia, Chris refused to get involved in a game of wit he knew he couldn't win. He said, "Where's Keanu?"

Mark was instantly transformed from comedian to cop, "Upstairs, on his bed."

Chris followed Mark through the door, his eyes roaming over the studio, hung with more of David Keanu's work. His eyes stopped in stunned surprise on a painting unlike any other in the studio.

"You like that painting?" Mark had come back to see what was keeping him.

"Yeah, I do."

The painting was of a woman standing on the platform of a *heiau*. Her skin was golden, shimmering in an ethereal light. A brief tapa sarong barely covered her below the waist, revealing almost all of one hip, where it was knotted at the side. Above the waist, she was naked. Tendrils of long, gently waving hair fell like molten strands of gold over the center of her beautiful breasts. Chris gasped audibly as he looked at the face of the beautiful woman, her lips parted sensuously, her amber eyes glowing with a deep and burning passion as her arms reached out in welcome, the long, graceful hands beckoning him into their embrace. It was Claudia—a Claudia Chris had perceived and had caught brief glimpses of. It was evident David had seen what Chris did in Claudia, and more.

"I want that painting."

"Which one?"

"You know which one."

"Does that mean you'd pay money for it?"

"Yes. I'd even pay money for it."

"It's Claudia, isn't it?"

"Yes. And I don't care what you have to do to get it. Just don't let it out of your sight until you bring it to me."

Mark grinned at him and shrugged. "You're a goner, man."

Chris grinned back and followed Mark up the stairs. Keanu's living area was one large room, like the studio below. Two lab people were dusting the nightstands on either side of the bed for fingerprints. Two more detectives were scrutinizing everything else in the room, and the police photographer was taking pictures.

Nothing seemed to have been disturbed, like it would have been if someone had broken in to rob Keanu. The king-size bed was against the far wall. Keanu was sprawled with his face up, wearing a pair of faded cutoffs, and a gold chain with a shark tooth around his neck, and nothing more. Even in death, he was a handsome man. Chris thought of Claudia in bed with Keanu and had to turn away. He saw Mark eyeing him and pretended to be looking for something on the nightstand next to the bed. There was nothing there. No needle, no powder; nothing.

"Okay, what's your scenario, Detective Mitsuro?"

"My theory is he didn't kill himself, intentionally or otherwise. There was some powder on the coffee table when we came in. He was probably already pretty well stoned and in bed when someone else came in. If you look at his arms, there are fresh punctures in both, but no needles."

"You checked all the garbage cans?"

"Yeah. I figure they dumped them down the toilet, or took the needles with them. We've got all the garbage bundled up for closer inspection, but there were no needles in it. He had some old needle tracks—so old they're scars. Only these two are fresh." He pointed to the new wounds on both arms. "I think he took most of his stuff through the nose, or smoked it. There are some joints around."

Chris frowned. He continued to look around, not liking the conclusions he was coming to. Mark and the lab people hadn't missed anything. That meant Mark was right in his analysis, and Claudia could be in danger, too.

"Did you get anything on that license plate number I called in yesterday?"

"Yeah. Belongs to Phnom Latmeong."

Chris nodded. That figured. Phnom Latmeong had connections all over the Orient. He had escaped the last Asian conflict, losing his money but not his connections. He made frequent business trips out of the state. He had a legitimate import business, but there was suspicion he also imported goods that were not so legitimate.

"What about Puna?"

"No one knows where he is."

Chris gave Mark a disgusted look.

"They think he and his brothers are out hunting."

"I hope you put out an APB on him."

"Yeah. I'll keep you posted."

He smiled at his protégé. "You do good work, Detective Mitsuro."

Mark smiled back and bowed. Chris chuckled and said, "And don't forget to take the painting. I don't want it destroyed."

It was after noon when Chris knocked on the door of Claudia's suite. He saw the peephole darken before she opened the door and let him in. He was holding a tray full of food.

"Hope you're hungry."

"I didn't think I was, but that smells good. What do you have here, anyway?"

"Two luncheon specials from the Tropical Garden. One special is Hawaiian-Thai chicken salad, and the other is Hawaiian ono. Which would you like?"

"The salad sounds good to me."

"I was hoping it would."

He uncovered the luncheon plates and handed her the salad. Hot, succulent hunks of marinated chicken with mandarin oranges and macadamia nuts covered a bed of crisp salad greens. He was glad to see that Claudia didn't hesitate to begin eating.

"This is good. And your fish looks good, too."

"Yeah, they're almost as good at cooking fish as I am."

That brought a smile to her face, and he smiled back. He would wait until she asked him about what he had found at David's studio.

He didn't want to alarm her. She needed to recover from the shock of David's death before she could deal with any more bad news.

"I have to go up to the station for a while this afternoon to file a report. You can go with me if you want."

"No. I'll be all right here. I can watch TV or read. It's okay."

"Whatever you feel most comfortable with. I'll bring something back for supper." He started piling his dishes onto the tray. Claudia finished her coffee and fitted her dishes into his. He rose with the tray and she went ahead of him to open the door.

He paused at the door and said, "Remember, don't let anyone in."

"I'll remember."

◆ ◆ ◆

Claudia was starting to worry when Chris finally returned with their supper.

"I'm sorry I took so long. Are you ready to eat?" She followed him to the table. He set down the tray, pulled the table away from the corner, and adjusted the louvers on the side windows to let in more air. The sun was setting the cloud layer on the crest of Lanai on fire. "Are you ready for pheasant under glass?"

She could no longer hold off asking about David's death. "No. I want to know what's going on."

His face sobered. "Let's eat while everything is still warm. I'll try to fill you in while we eat."

Claudia sat down, and Chris handed her a plate of garlic-buttered scampi and Polynesian rice. "This looks delicious."

"It's as good as it looks."

She cut one of the large shrimp and daintily placed it in her mouth, smiling at the taste of the delicious morsel. "Mmm. This is wonderful. By the way, who is paying for these gourmet meals you're bringing me?"

"I wish I could say it was Maui County tax dollars at work."

"Oh, Chris, this is coming out of your pocket, isn't it? You don't have to do this. I can buy my meals."

"You are in my custody. That means I'm responsible for you. I'll send in a voucher to the department. Does that make it better?"

"Well, maybe. But you make me feel guilty for eating so well."

"Don't. You were treated rotten yesterday, and then you got seasick. Just call it getting even."

She smiled at that and ate the second half of her shrimp. Between bites, she reminded him, "You were going to tell me what you found out today."

He swallowed a forkful of rice and answered, "I found out who owns the car you gave me the license number for. It belongs to a businessman here in Lahaina. He owns several shops and imports a lot of jewelry and other gift items from all over the orient. We suspected he was also involved in drugs, but we've never had anything on him until now."

"What about Puna?"

"They didn't find him or his brothers at their home. Mark put out an APB on him. It's possible either Puna or Phnom knew we picked you up. Either one of them could have had someone watching you at the airport."

"And Rosa?"

"The LA police picked her up, but she was clean. They couldn't hold her without any evidence. If she'd actually had the suitcase in her possession, they could have booked her."

"And what about this other man?"

"We are hoping we'll find some evidence indicating he was involved in David's death."

She put down her fork. "You mean David was murdered?"

"It looks that way."

She closed her eyes and shuddered. Chris reached across the table and took her hand. "Claudia, I didn't want to tell you like this. I'm sorry."

She opened her eyes, swiped at tears that trembled on her eyelids, and said, "It's okay. I'm fine."

He released her hand. She picked up her fork again and finished eating. Finally, she said, "Do you think Puna would kill David?"

"No. More likely, Phnom is involved in it."

"Then Puna could be dead, too?"

"He could be. Like I said, if it is Phnom, he won't want witnesses."

Now she was afraid. "What are we going to do?"

"Whatever it takes to keep you safe."

"But you don't have any evidence against Phnom."

"We have your testimony. We've got an arrest warrant out for him now. Unfortunately, he happens to be off the island on a business trip."

"But I didn't see his face well enough to make a positive identification."

"We'll make sure you can identify him."

Claudia was beginning to lose her appetite. This just kept getting worse as she learned more. How could she possibly live with herself if she lied and she was wrong? She knotted her hands in her lap to keep them from shaking. "So, where does that leave me?"

"I don't want you worrying, Claudia. Mark will call me as soon as something else turns up. Until then, let me do the worrying."

◆ ◆ ◆

The next morning, Chris had just brought up breakfast and placed it on the table when his cell phone rang.

"Yes?"

Claudia watched his face. She saw the smile on his face at hearing Mark's voice disappear. He set his jaw, and two lines formed between his eyebrows in consternation. When his eyes met hers they were dark and worried.

"Okay, Mark. I'm going to go with our alternate plan."

He ended the call and looked at her, concern etched in the lines of his face.

"They've found Puna and his brothers." He paused. "I don't know how to tell you this without scaring you. They're dead."

She felt drained. "How? Where?"

Chris took a long swallow of the cooling coffee and answered, "They located his pickup late yesterday on the back side of Haleakala. It had gone off the road and rolled down the mountain several hundred feet. They were able to get down to it this morning. Puna and his brothers were in it. They'd been shot."

She closed her eyes for a long moment, willing herself to remain calm as she locked her hands together in her lap. "What is the alternate plan?"

"I'm going to take you back to Wailuku. I can't protect you here. I want you in protective custody twenty-four-seven."

He turned his attention to his phone and punched in some numbers. After a few moments he said, "Hi, Glenn. This is Chris Hadley, Maui Police Department. How soon are you expecting that weather front to hit us?"

There was silence for a few moments before he asked, "How severe is this thing going to be?"

He turned grim eyes on Claudia, and she felt her heart constrict in her chest. She heard the palm trees rustling in the wind outside. She separated the drape enough to see the sky to the south of Lanai. Banks of dark clouds were building. They boiled in an angry mass as they spread across the horizon.

Chris put down the phone and said, "Better eat. We're going to have to get out of here. There's a pretty severe weather front coming in from the South Pacific. We're going to have a lot of wind and rain. I want to be out of here before it hits."

Claudia didn't feel hungry. She forced herself to eat the papaya and muffin Chris had brought for breakfast. She drank the coffee and juice. The wind was really picking up now. The fronds on the palm trees were clattering together like bamboo drumsticks as they whipped in the gusting wind.

Between bites of his breakfast he told her, "Better wear slacks and your tennies. If you've got a hooded sweatshirt, bring it with you."

She had a sinking feeling in her stomach; she suspected he wasn't telling her everything. "How are you planning on taking me to Wailuku?"

His eyes were blue steel as he looked at her. "There's only one way I can take you and be sure we won't be followed, get stuck in a traffic jam, or be stranded because of road closures. We're not going to take your bags, so get what you need and can carry easily in something small. I can have Mark get your suitcases later. We're going to walk over to the harbor. I'm leaving my car here, just in case there is someone watching it." He paused, then added, "Pack your ammo. I want you to carry your gun."

Claudia rose from the table and went to get the things she would need. She put them in a canvas bag she used as a beach tote. She slipped her derringer into her pocket and put extra shells in her other pocket. She packed the hooded sweatshirt from her suitcase. Chris was putting his things in the bag he'd brought from his boat. He pulled a shoulder holster and gun from the bag, slipped it on, and put a windbreaker on over his shirt.

"Are you ready to go?"

Never feeling less ready in her life, she answered, "Yes."

CHAPTER XIV

They left the room and went down the service stairs leading to the employee entrance into the kitchen area on the north side of the building. The kitchen was busy. Cooks and waitresses greeted Chris as he passed through with Claudia. They went out the secured backdoor onto the delivery dock and the driveway leading to the employee parking garage next to Kahoma Stream. They crossed Front Street and walked down the road toward Mala Wharf. The wind was growing stronger by the minute, whipping leaves off trees and picking up red dirt from the graveyard next to the beach. Chris was all business now. His eyes scanned everything as they walked toward the wind-whipped water.

They got to the ramp, and Chris told her, "Hang on to my hand and step where I step."

He held his hand out to her and she took it, not liking the idea of traversing the rocky revetment and being splashed with each choppy wave rolling into shore. Chris went slowly, holding her hand tightly and keeping her from falling on the slippery rocks.

In less than five minutes, Claudia was climbing into the rubber raft. Chris untied the line holding the raft and stepped in behind her. He pulled the starter rope, and the little outboard motor sputtered and died. Chris pulled the rope again, and this time the engine caught. He backed the raft out into the capping water. Claudia's stomach was tight with fear as the raft was buffeted by the wind and choppy waves.

She almost felt relief when Chris nosed the raft into the back of the sailboat. The boat was bobbing like a cork on the roughening water, and Claudia could almost feel herself get seasick just looking at it. Fortunately, she had remembered to take her Dramamine when Chris mentioned their escape route. Chris secured the rubber raft to the back of the sailboat and reached out for Claudia, his grip on her hand strong and reassuring. She stepped gingerly toward the boarding ladder on the boat, and Chris was there to steady her as she climbed up the pitching transom. She braced herself with a hand on the boom of the sailboat, moving out of Chris's way as he came on deck after her.

"Put these bags in the galley. I'm going to get the engine started. Then I'm going to teach you how to sail this boat."

She looked at him with wide eyes, feeling less certain with each heartbeat about what he was expecting her to do. She wanted to protest. She wanted to say she couldn't do what he was asking her to do, but she didn't. She didn't have a choice.

When she came back up on deck, Chris had the floor opened up over the inboard engine and was checking the oil and spark plugs. He squirted something into places she couldn't see. In a few minutes, he stood up, went to the wheel, inserted a key in the panel behind the wheel, and turned it. The engine turned over but didn't catch. He tried it again, and still it failed to start. He went back to the engine, took something apart, and squirted the spray he had been using into it. He screwed the cap down, returned to the wheel, and tried the key again. After two more tries, the engine caught hold with a deep throb. Chris, a hint of relief passing over his face, replaced the door over the engine compartment and stood up.

"Okay, First Mate Jordan. I need to free us from the anchor buoys. I want you to man the wheel and keep us from going toward shore. Aim the boat at the open water as soon as you feel it start to drift toward shore when I release the bow line."

"You're sure I can do this?"

"I know you can. It drives just like a car. Now take hold of the wheel and show her who's boss."

Claudia took hold of the wheel.

"This lever on the side is the throttle. Just ease it forward gently to give it more power. Got it?"

She looked at him, feeling panicked.

He put his arm around her shoulder and said softly, "You can do it. You've got to do it."

He went to the back of the boat. As soon as he unsnapped the line holding it to the aft buoy, she felt the boat swing stern first toward the shore. Chris, surefooted and lithe as a monkey in a tree, went along the narrow catwalk beside the cabin house to the front deck. He lay down on his stomach to reach the line holding the boat to the forward buoy. Claudia tensed as she felt the boat come free and start to turn in the wind and waves. She turned the wheel, and feeling no response, she gripped the throttle and gently pushed it forward. The engine responded, and the nose came around and pushed into the waves. Chris jumped down beside her and encircled her with his arms, his hands over hers on the wheel helping her guide the boat out into open water.

In a few minutes, they were away from shore. Chris said into her ear, his breath warm against her cheek, "Hold her steady. I'm going to get the sails up."

The strength and warmth of him left her, and she had to work harder to hold the wheel now that his hands weren't there to help. She watched Chris raise the sails while trying to keep the boat headed toward the darkening shore of Molokai as the gusting winds hit them. She could feel the strain on her wrists as she fought the wheel.

The moment the wind filled the sails, the boat seemed to leap forward like an uncoiled spring. It frightened Claudia, as it seemed to take on a life of its own, straining to be free like a wild, unbroken horse. The boom over her head started groaning as it tried to break the line holding it. Chris was back, and she welcomed the feel of his arms around her as he took the strain off her tiring arms and aching wrists. He reached for the key and turned off the engine. The throbbing stopped, and there was nothing but the rush of the wind and water surrounding them.

"Want to rest for a while?"

She turned her face so her voice would reach his ear before being snatched away by the wind. "Yes."

He took the wheel from her and said, "In the cupboard under the table seat there are life jackets. Get them out, put one on, and bring me the one with my name on it."

She went down the steps into the cabin. She had to hang on to keep from losing her balance as the boat rose and fell with the power of the wind and waves. She got down on her hands and knees to find the life jackets. She pulled them out, putting one on and stowing the rest of them, except for the one with Chris's name on the back. She took it on deck to him and held the wheel while he fastened it about himself.

Claudia sat down on a step of the ladder to the deck and watched the storm advance toward them. A black veil of rain had obliterated the gray mass of Kahoolawe and was overtaking Lanai. While Claudia watched, the day grew darker and darker, and she felt the first wind-driven drops of rain hit her face. The wind began to scream through the rigging, and Claudia clung tightly to the railing, too frightened to even be seasick.

Chris yelled, "Come take the wheel."

Claudia felt the wind hit her with driving force as she stood up. It pushed her into Chris. He grabbed her and pulled her into the security of his arms. She welcomed the feel of him, not wanting to be out of the circle of his arms even for a moment.

"I've got to take in sail. The wind's getting too strong. Hold her right where she is."

She took hold of the wheel. He held it with her for a long moment, and then asked, "Got it?"

She nodded. She felt him leave her, and the wheel wrenched in her hands. She fought it back and looked in panic for Chris. He was already on the forward deck. His mouth formed words, but the wind whipped them away. She used all her strength to hold the wheel in the position he wanted. As soon as he had adjusted the sail, the boat settled.

Chris jumped down off the deck and took the wheel out of Claudia's straining hands. She was to the point of not being able to hold it, and her arms trembled with weakness when she relinquished the wheel. She wondered how long he would be able to fight it.

She sat down on the deck, out of the wind, but the rain still found her. It enveloped them and soaked them with stinging force. She closed her eyes against the pelting rain, rubbing her aching arms, vowing silently to never set foot on a boat again.

For hours, the storm battered them with its force, driving the sailboat relentlessly through the wind-blown chop and white-capped waves. When she looked up again, Chris was steering the boat with one hand while rubbing his upper arm with his free hand.

"What's wrong? Are you tired? Do you need a break?"

"Yeah. I don't usually sail in conditions like this. I thought we could beat it and get around the point and down to Kahului harbor before it caught us."

Claudia stepped between Chris's arms and gripped the wheel. He stood behind her rubbing his arms shielding her with his body against the onslaught of rain. When she glanced at him he was looking landward.

"What are you looking for?"

"I am hoping we are close to rounding Nakalele Point. We have one chance for a place to put in for the night if we can find it."

"Where's that?"

"Kahakuloa bay."

Just then Claudia felt a shift in the wind that made the boat shudder as the wind from the windward side of the island deflected the headland winds coming from the east.

Chris yelled. "That's it! We're past Nakalele Point. Stay with the wheel. I need to adjust the sails."

When Chris came down from the deck he went into the cabin and came back with binoculars and studied the shoreline, leaning against the rail just behind Claudia. She looked toward the shore, too, but it looked like an indeterminate wall a darker shade of gray than the steady downpour of rain enveloping them.

"What are you looking for?"

"There's a blowhole out there somewhere. If I can find it, I'll know where we are. Can you keep the wheel for a while longer?"

"I think so. It doesn't seem to be as hard to manage now."

"Let me know when you get tired."

Claudia hung on to the wheel, keeping it turned away from the landmass that loomed in the distance. She was soaked to the skin, and now that she was standing up where the wind could hit her, she was beginning to feel cold. She didn't know her teeth were chattering until she felt Chris's arms around her. His hands were rubbing her arms.

She stuttered, "Did you find it yet?"

"No, but you're getting cold. You want to go into the cabin and get into my sleeping bag?"

"That would be worse. At least I'm not seasick out here."

His hands left her arms and she felt him lift the heavy mass of wet, tangled hair off her neck and place his lips against her skin.

"Chris, what are you doing?" Her teeth had stopped chattering.

He moved his lips across the back of her neck to the other side, and answered, "Trying to get you warmed up."

"What about your blowhole? I thought you had to find it."

"I do, but at least I made your teeth stop chattering."

Claudia felt her hair fall against her neck but Chris kept one arm around her, shielding her from the wind while he scanned the shoreline with his binoculars.

Finally, he breathed a sigh of relief and said, "There it is."

"The blowhole?"

"Yes. Take a look."

Chris took the wheel in the hand that had been holding her and gave her the binoculars. She braced herself against him, held on to the binoculars with both hands, and looked at the gray mass, suddenly distinguishable through the power of the binoculars. The high black cliffs took shape, and a large, flattened point of rock jutted out into the angry water. As she watched, a frothing wave hit the rock, sending a plume of water shooting through the hole. The wind whipped the water, spraying the black cliffs behind it. She kept the glasses to her eyes until another wave broke over the rock and it spouted again like a geyser.

"I never knew this was here."

"It's hard to see from the road, especially when the ocean isn't strong enough to push the water through the rocks."

"Now that you've found it, what does it mean?"

"It means we're getting closer to the bay where we can put in for the night."

She breathed, "Thank God. Are you sure you can find it?"

"I hope so. You keep watching the shoreline and let me know what you see. I'll take us in closer."

She stayed braced against him, nestled between his arms, one leg securely anchored between his legs. She felt his arms move against her as he turned the wheel, causing warm sensations to reach her skin in spite of the wet and cold.

"All I see is cliffs and rocks."

"Keep watching."

She kept watching, looking so hard for something resembling a bay her eyes began to blur. She took the binoculars away from her face and rested a moment.

"What's wrong?"

"I'm looking too hard."

He chuckled and said, "It's not that hard to find."

She put the binoculars up again and swept them across the cliffs, looming closer and higher as Chris guided the boat toward them. Then she saw it—a break in the cliffs.

"I think I see it. You'd better look."

He took the glasses from her, and she turned to take the wheel from him.

"Yes. That's it. Keep the wheel. I'm going to start the engine and take in the sail."

He hung the binoculars around her neck. With one hand on the wheel with hers, he turned the key, and the engine throbbed to life. "You'll need to give it power when I get the sail down."

Before she even had time to answer, he was headed for the deck and beginning to take down the sails. Claudia felt the abrupt drop in power as the boat settled. She pushed the throttle to keep them moving toward the shore.

Chris was back and stood behind her, his body breaking the wind. His arms encircled her, and his hands rubbed her arms until she felt warmth replace the numbing cold. His fingers worked up to her shoulders to massage the aching muscles there. Then he gripped the wheel and guided the boat into the little bay nestled between the black ridges of the mountain.

Leaning against Chris as they headed for the wave-washed crescent of shore between the abutments of black rock rising on each side of the bay, Claudia realized how tired she was, how tense she was, and how wet and cold she was. If anyplace looked like paradise to her, the tiny native village of Kahakuloa was it. In the fast-fading light, she could see rooftops among wind-tossed palms, boats pulled up high off the wave-battered beach, and a patch of lush grass in front of a large building, where discarded cars were rusting away and several boats rested on wooden cradles.

Claudia saw some men coming around the building, followed by a large dog. They were heading toward a gate in the fence running from the front corner of the building to intersect with another fence running up the slope past some houses.

Chris cut the engine as they neared the beach and let the waves carry the boat into the gray, rocky beach.

He ordered, "Brace yourself against the wheel."

Claudia held onto the wheel with a death grip and tried to swallow the fear that was welling up inside her like the wind churned waves crashing against the darkened shore.

◆   ◆   ◆

Chris used his body to press Claudia against the wheel, holding her tight. They hit with a jarring thud that whipped them both with the force of a rear-end collision.

The boat heeled over as another wave slammed into it. Chris yelled at Claudia, "Get up on the deck and jump."

He pushed Claudia toward the ladder to the deck and followed her, hanging on to the strap of her life jacket to keep her from falling as they scrambled along the cabin and across the steeply canted deck. Chris let go of Claudia as they got to the edge of the deck. Another wave rocked the boat, and Claudia pitched off the deck, landing spread-eagle on her face in the receding water.

Chris grabbed the anchor, hurled it out onto the rocks, jumped down beside her, and yelled, "Claudia, are you all right?"

There was no response. He turned her over. Her eyes were closed, and he knew a moment of heart-wrenching fear as he felt for the pulse in her neck. It was strong and steady. She was just stunned. He picked her up in his arms as another wave came charging onto the beach, and carried her toward the grassy area beyond the rocks. The large rottweiler-cross dog came bounding across the grass toward him.

A familiar voice yelled against the wind and rain, "Well, Mr. Christian, you chose one bloody hell of a storm to mutiny in."

"Hello, Jack. How are you?"

"Bloody hell better than you. Who's that in your arms?"

"Claudia Jordan."

Jack's eyes narrowed. "And just what the hell are you doing sailing about in this weather?"

"Police business."

Jack frowned. "I supposed that means you can't tell me what's going on?"

Chris smiled grimly, "That's right. This is strictly on a need to know basis."

"Do I need to know if we're in danger?"

"I hope not. Can you help us out?"

"Ye don't even need to ask. What can we do?"

Claudia was coming to, and he lowered her to her feet and supported her with his arms. The dog circled Claudia, sniffing her from the ground up.

"Brutus, knock it off," Jack ordered. The dog backed off and came to stand in front of Chris, wagging his tail in recognition.

"Jack, this is Claudia. Claudia, this is Aussie Jack."

◆ ◆ ◆

Claudia lifted a limp hand, and Jack took it in both of his strong, rough hands and shook it, saying, "She's one bloody beauty, isn't she?"

Chris grinned. "Yeah, even looking like a drowned rat." Then he added, "These are Jack's sons, Kimo and Koma. Kimo is the one who looks like Jack."

Claudia shook hands with the boys. She saw a resemblance between Kimo and Jack, but Kimo was taller and a few shades darker than his father. Koma was even darker, taller, and much heavier than either of them.

Jack asked, "You want to save the bloody boat?"

"Yeah."

Jack turned to his two tall, husky sons and said, "Go get the truck and the winch, boys." Then, to Chris, he asked, "You got anything on there you need?"

"There's a couple of bags with some dry clothes in the galley."

"I'll get 'em when the boys get the bloody thing on a cradle. Now we better get you up to the house. I'll get the fire going under the hot tub and get Lucky to make you some hot coffee. How long since you've eaten?"

"Not since this morning."

"Lucky made a fresh pot of fish soup today. I'll have her warm it up. Well, come on. Let's get out of this bloody wind and rain."

Chris kept his arm around Claudia as they followed Aussie Jack through the tall, wet grass toward the gate, Brutus trotting along ahead of them. Jack's boys had the truck started and were coming around the corner of the big building and headed along the fence toward the gate. They stood aside while the truck went through the gate and continued on past the building.

There were no lights anywhere, but it looked like there was more than one dwelling structure up the hill from the building. With the wind whipping the palms and the rain beating a tattoo against the metal roofs of the buildings, it all appeared eerie to Claudia.

They followed Aussie Jack to the low end of the first building, and he yelled as they neared the upper structure, "Hey, Lucky. We got company. Put on the coffee and light a bloody lantern." In a quieter voice, he told Chris and Claudia, "Bloody damn lights went out this afternoon. Must be a bloody slide up on the road."

He fumbled for something on a post and switched on a battery-operated lantern. He began throwing chunks of wood into a large, sheet-iron lined box under what Claudia thought looked like a bathhouse. He stuffed in some dry tinder and struck a match to it. "You'll have hot water quick enough. Now let's get you up to the house."

They followed him up the steps. A lantern was lit on the large porch. A tall, husky woman in a long muumuu was adding wood to the big, ovenlike structure. The walls of the oven were mortared rock, and the top was covered with a thick sheet of metal. She turned as they came onto the porch, a smile on her broad, beautiful face.

Jack said, "This is my wife, Lucky." He put an arm around the woman, who was taller and outweighed him by a good fifty pounds, and added with a grin, "Well, her name is really Luke, but I call her Lucky, because it was the luckiest bloody day of my life when I found this bay and met her." He gave her a squeeze and continued, "You remember Inspector Hadley, don't you, dearie?"

Luke's smile broadened as she said, "Yes, Detective Sergeant Hadley. Welcome." Her speech and diction were perfect.

Chris took up the introductions, "And this is Claudia, Luke."

Luke smiled and said, "Welcome, Claudia. I'm warming coffee. Stay here by the fire while I get some cups."

Luke padded on bare feet into the kitchen beyond a half-wall of wood separating the porch from the house. The front part of the kitchen, looking down the slope, was also open, with large, louvered, folding shutters that could be closed against the storm. Luke pulled them shut and fastened them against the rain and wind. Chris and Claudia moved toward the fire. Chris released his hold on Claudia, started unsnapping the hooks on his life vest, and shrugged out of it. Jack hung it on a line running between the posts of the covered porch. Claudia attempted to remove hers, but her fingers were so cold and stiff she only got one snap undone before Chris finished the rest of them and helped her out of it.

Luke brought the cups, poured coffee, and said, "Jack, bring the bench here by the fire for them to sit on."

Jack and Chris moved the bench closer to the fire and they sat, curling cold hands around the warm mugs of coffee Luke handed them.

Claudia found her voice and said, "Thank you, Luke."

Jack said, "I'd better go down and see if I can help the boys. Lucky will get you fixed up for the tub. I'll be back with your bags."

Luke followed him down the steps and went to light a lantern on the deck of the other building. Claudia could see in the glow of the light that the building was indeed a bathhouse. Luke disappeared inside a door for a few moments. She came out and went in another door. When she appeared again, she went across the deck and got down on her knees to test the warmth of the water in the tub.

She ascended the steps to the porch and said, "The water is warm now. I left you towels and kimonos. Please enjoy when you are ready."

Chris stood up and smiled at their gracious hostess. "Thank you, Luke. Come on, Claudia, let's go get warm."

She followed Chris down the steps to the deck of the bathhouse. Mirrors in unique, hand-carved frames hung on either side of the bathhouse doors. Claudia touched the beautifully carved frames, feeling the velvet-smooth wood, and asked, "Who did these?"

"Jack. He likes to work with wood in his spare time."

Claudia opened the door to one of the rooms and went in. With only the lantern light from outside, she could barely see the towel and kimono on a bench inside the room. She started removing her wet clothes.

Then the lantern light went out, and Chris said, "I'm going in the tub. Come on out when you're ready."

Claudia heard him sigh in pleasure as he got into the tub. "This is great, Claudia."

Claudia finished undressing, opened the door, and stepped out onto the deck. The cool, wind-driven rain hit her naked body as she stood on the deck. She felt her skin prickle with gooseflesh, and the nipples of her breasts spring to life. There was something erotic about standing there in the dark, knowing Chris was looking at her. She felt a thrill of expectation course through her as she remembered how many times during the long, harrowing day he had put his arms around her and held her, his lips against her neck, his breath warm against her ear. Now she wanted to be able to fulfill those promised intimacies. She no longer felt shame or guilt for how she had acted—for what she had asked him to do. He had not said or done anything to remind her of that afternoon. He acted as if it had never happened. And his actions today—the way he had held her; the way he had rubbed her aching arms and massaged her tired shoulders—were tender, thoughtful acts of someone who cared deeply for her.

The words *cared deeply for her* echoed in her mind, and she suddenly knew the truth. She wondered why he hadn't said something, and then she knew why he hadn't. He had told her himself. She was David Keanu's friend. And she had still loved David. But the reality was that David was gone, and nothing could change that.

Claudia looked down at the large, black rectangle set in the corner of the deck and shielded against the wind by wooden walls. She saw no steps into the dull, dark sheen of the water. "What's the best way for me to get in?"

"Sit down on the edge, and you should be able to feel the bottom of the tub with your feet. It's not that deep."

She sat down on the edge of the deck and lowered herself into the tub, disappearing into the dark water. "Oh my God! This is heaven!" She settled into the warm tub and sat on the wood-slatted bottom, feeling the heat radiate up through the metal bottom from the fire below. She let the warmth of the water seep into every chilled inch of her body. She sat with her knees bent, careful to avoid Chris. It wasn't that she didn't want his warmth and tenderness. She was afraid of what that contact would lead to.

Feeling the electricity between them and wanting to divert it, she asked, "How did you meet Jack?"

"There was some trouble here about ten years ago. I was still a rookie and didn't know why they sent the rookies out to work on these village problems. What they knew and I didn't was no one ever got anywhere with the natives, especially haole cops.

"Jack had been living here about fifteen years by then. He was a surfer from Australia in perpetual search of a bigger wave. He finally ended up in Hawaii, and then Maui. The waves get really big on the top of the island when we get a storm like we've got now. That's how he found Kahakuloa Bay and Luke. He married her, and he hasn't gone in search of a bigger wave since."

"And did you take care of the trouble?"

"It's more like Jack took care of the trouble. The trouble they were having was being caused by a couple of local boys. They were getting into people's houses and stealing stuff, but nobody wanted to say anything because they're all family here.

"They got into Jack's boat shop one night. Jack heard them, trapped them in there, and found out who they were. When I got down here to talk to everybody, Jack was the only one who'd talk to me. He was haole. He wasn't part of the family, and he wasn't going to put up with what those two teenagers were doing. He told me who the culprits were.

"I went to the families of the boys involved, let them know I knew who they were, and the problem stopped. Because of Luke, there was no retaliation. Now Jack is kind of the village head here. He's the mediator and representative for the whole village. He's kind of a one-man city council and mayor."

"And Luke? She's beautiful. And educated."

"Yes. She was sent to the boarding school in Lahaina and then went to Maui Community College. She worked in Wailuku as a legal secretary, but this is her ancestral home. When she married Jack, they made Kahakuloa their home."

Jack's voice, close behind Claudia, startled her. "You blokes turned into bloody prunes yet?"

Chris answered, "Not quite yet. Did you get the boat off the beach?"

"Piece of cake. I put your bags up in the guest cottage. Come on up to the house when you get done. Lucky's got the soup warming."

"We'll be up in a few minutes."

Jack chuckled and said, "Take as long as you need."

Claudia blushed and was glad Chris couldn't see her. She turned her face up and let the rain run down her flushed cheeks, feeling the power of Chris's attraction to her now that she recognized the truth of it. The response it was kindling in her was undeniable. She stood up, sat on the edge of the tub, and swung her legs out of the water. She couldn't stay in the tub with him any longer and not touch him.

"Are you ready to get out?"

"Yes. I'm so hungry I could die." But it wasn't the hunger for food she was thinking of. She went into the dressing room, felt for the towel on the bench, and dried herself off, luxuriating in finally being warm after hours in the soaking, wind-chilled rain. The lantern flared to life, and she knew Chris was out of the tub. She put on the kimono wrap Luke had left for her and made a carryall out of the towel for her wet clothes. She carefully dried her gun and bullets and placed them within easy reach in the bundle. She stayed inside, waiting for Chris, the rain a gentle whisper on the metal roof.

She heard his door open, and she came out of her dressing room. The look on his face before he turned off the lantern was filled with all the expectation she was feeling. His eyes traveled to where the kimono neckline met in the valley between her breasts.

He took her hand, and they ran barefoot through the rain, up the steps to the beckoning lantern in the kitchen of Jack's house. Luke was stirring the iron kettle resting on the thick, metal plate over the fire. She lifted it off with a thick potholder and carried it to the table. Chris and Claudia followed her.

"Please, sit down."

Claudia slid along the bench until there was enough room for Chris to sit beside her. Luke ladled hot soup into bowls and set them in front of her guests. Then she passed a basket of warm, fragrant bread to them.

"Would you like more coffee?"

Chris answered, "Yes, please."

Jack was still muscular, with only a slight paunch at the waist. He settled across the table from Chris and asked, "Does anybody know where you are?"

"No. We left rather suddenly."

"How about your phone?"

"It's on the boat. I can try it tomorrow. Could you tell if the boat suffered any damage?"

"Naw, it was getting' too dark by the time we got it off the rocks."

"If we can't use the boat, could I get you to drive us into town tomorrow?"

Jack frowned, and the weathered skin of his face resembled leather in the lamplight. "I can take you as far as we can get in the truck, but I know bloody well there's a slide someplace on the road between here and Wailuku. You was goin' to Wailuku, wasn't you?"

"Yes."

Luke set coffee in front of Claudia and said, "Hush, Jack, and let them eat. You can ask questions tomorrow."

Jack only let Chris take a few spoons of soup before he asked, "How long since you've had that boat out of the water?"

"I've never had it out of the water. I don't know how long it was in the water before I bought it."

"It's got a lot of barnacle growth on it. I'd say it's in need of a good cleaning and painting. I can tell you more after I see it in daylight. You want to do it as long as we got it out of the water?"

"Sure. I know you and the boys will do a good job. You can give me a call at the station when you get it done, and I can have Mark bring me up to get it."

Claudia finished her soup and said, "That was delicious, Luke. Thank you."

Luke smiled and asked, "Is there anything more I can get you?"

Claudia said, "I'm fine."

Chris echoed, "Me, too, Luke. Thank you. This will hold us until morning."

Jack got up and said, "Well, since you seem so bloody anxious to get to bed, I might as well see you to the guesthouse."

He took a flashlight off the counter behind him and said, "Right this way."

Claudia wondered how the attraction she was feeling for Chris could be so obvious to anyone else. What signals was she putting out that could be so easily read? She wondered if Chris was reading her as well as Jack seemed to be. Or was it the way Chris treated her? And the way she took his hand, or accepted his arm around her? That must be it. It was plain to everyone but her.

CHAPTER XV

Jack opened the door to the guesthouse and shone the light around the room, flashing it across the hand-carved wooden bedstead with a handmade, quilted coverlet on top, then over the wooden, louvered doors that opened to the bay and across the beautifully carved chest on the wall opposite the bed, where their bags were. "The loo is in the corner to the left; the closet is to the right. Have a good night."

Chris answered, "We'll see you in the morning. Good night."

Claudia walked to the louvered, folding doors at the end of the room and opened them. The wind had dropped and the rain had slackened while they had been eating. There was just the sound of the storm-wild ocean surging against the beach. She felt Chris behind her even before he spoke her name.

"Claudia." It was a whispered plea, soft and poignant against her ear.

She answered, "Yes." Her heart was thumping with expectancy inside her chest.

Claudia's soft response was all the answer he needed. He put his arms around her, gently pulling her against him. Claudia yielded. He brushed the heavy weight of her still-damp hair aside, pushed the kimono off her shoulder, and left a burning trail of kisses from her ear to the point of her shoulder before he whispered, "I want you with all my heart and soul."

She turned in his arms, her arms going around his neck, her fingers curling into his hair as she lifted her lips to his, swaying into him, feeling the fire in him and wanting the fire of him inside her.

Chris lifted her off her feet, carried her to the bed, and placed her reverently on the quilted coverlet. He lay down beside her, his hand pulling loose the sash holding the kimono closed. His lips found her hard, taut nipples and caressed them until Claudia pulled his mouth back up to hers, writhing against him in desperate need to have all of him.

He pressed his knee against her legs, and she parted her thighs for him. She felt heated moisture erupt inside her at the touch of his leg. Her mouth was searing his while her hands freed the belt of his kimono and pushed it off his shoulders. She moved her lips to his naked shoulders and chest, running her fingers through the curls of blond hair she couldn't see but remembered so well.

Chris gathered her to him and whispered against her ear, "No regrets?"

Claudia's answer was to slide her hand between their bodies and caress him. He caught her hand, brought it to his lips, and kissed each trembling finger. Then, in a voice vibrating with passion, he whispered, "Stay right where you are." He lifted his body from hers and started to get off the bed.

Claudia gripped his hand. "Where are you going?"

"I want to protect you."

She hung on to his hand and whispered, "It's okay. I'm protected."

He turned back to her, fitting his body against hers again. "Are you sure?"

She touched his face with her hand and smiled. "Very sure."

She pulled his head down to hers and kissed him. He groaned with pleasure and pressed her to the bed, covering her with his body. She opened for him and rose to meet him with her hips, his breath hot in her mouth, gasping as she took him into the volcano, into the very center of Pele's fire.

When they lay still wrapped in the afterglow of their passion, Claudia's chin was resting on Chris's shoulder, her lips against his neck, completely relaxed. Chris's arm was still around her, holding her and his other hand was caressing her breast, his thumb stroking her nipple. Claudia felt her nipple swell and harden at his touch and she breathed deeply of his scent and caressed his neck with her lips, content. She felt his hand leave her breast and gently brush the length of her body before he brought his hand to her jaw, tracing it with his fingers, lifting it until her lips were within reach. He kissed her tenderly.

Just before Claudia fell asleep, she heard Chris whisper against her lips. "I love you."

◆　　◆　　◆

Claudia awoke to the light coming in through the doors to the bay she had opened the night before. She had changed positions during the night, but she was still within the circle of Chris's arms. She felt the warmth of him and of his breath against her neck. She felt so complete, so happy, that she never wanted to leave this time and this place. She couldn't wait for him to wake up, and she turned to face him. She kissed him on the lips, teasing the inside of his mouth with her tongue.

His eyes came sleepily open and looked at her with wonder. She pressed her breasts against him and angled her leg over his hip, rubbing her foot against the backs of his thighs. He rolled onto his back and pulled her on top of him. Claudia settled over him feeling him come to life beneath her. She opened herself to him and felt the exquisite pleasure of him filling her. She gloried in the ride, feeling like a tigress freed from the cage that had held her prisoner to a man and a love that was gone. She felt Chris's lips caressing her neck and shoulders as his hands caressed her body, lingering on her full breasts. She savored every touch, taste and scent of him, wanting to lock the memory of him into her heart, mind and body. She didn't know what this day would bring, she didn't even know if she would ever see him again, but whatever happened she would have this moment in time for the rest of her life.

He whispered softly against her hair. "Will you marry me? I want to spend the rest of my life with you."

She raised her head, searching his clear blue eyes. They revealed to her all his hopes, his dreams, and his love. She gazed at him tenderly, glowing with happiness. She bent to kiss him, feeling something well up inside her choking off her response. It was too soon. Too soon.

"Is that a yes?"

"Oh, Chris. Right now I want nothing more in the world than to be with you. I want to stay right here and feel this happy for the rest of my life. But we're not home free yet."

She saw the hopes and dreams in his eyes fade, but the love remained. He acknowledged, "I'm sorry. You're right. I shouldn't have asked. I've loved you since the day I saw you walk into the hotel. There is no question in my mind, but I know you have to find answers to a lot of your own questions before you can give me an answer."

She caressed his face with her hand. He caught her hand in his and kissed her palm. She bent to kiss the back of his hand and said, "I'd better get decent."

He released her, and she scrambled off the bed, wrapped the kimono around her, and went to close the doors. She gazed out at the huge waves rolling in to break on the beach of speckled gray and white rocks. She saw Jack and his two tall, brown sons, one a milk-chocolate replica of Jack; the other, with Luke's build and darker chocolate skin, making Jack look small in comparison. They were going over Chris's boat with scrapers, chinking off the barnacles and loose paint.

She closed the doors, but adjusted the louvers to let in light and air. She came back to stand beside the bed, feeling guilty she had not told Chris how she felt. What she was feeling had come so suddenly she didn't know if she dared believe in it. She was afraid it might be a reaction to everything that had happened. Once she was through this terrible experience, she might not feel as she did now. But as she looked down at him and saw the tender, loving look in his eyes and felt the warmth, love, and security—the complete calmness and goodness of him—she knew what she was seeing and feeling was not an illusion. She sat down on the bed and took his hand.

"I want to give you more, Chris. I have been hurting for so long because of David, I didn't think I could ever love again. In twenty-four hours, you have changed everything. You have been patient, kind, and understanding. It has made me realize what a wonderful man you are and how lucky I am that you care for me." She hesitated uncertainly for a moment. "But I need time to sort everything out before I can be positive if what I'm feeling for you is real, or just a grateful response to your concern for me. I hope you can understand."

"Claudia, I will do whatever I have to do and wait as long as it takes for you to work it out."

She raised his hand to her lips and kissed the fingers that had so recently and so lovingly caressed her.

She rose, turned away from the bed, and went to retrieve her bag from the chest, admiring the beautiful wood and intricate carving even more in the light of day. She heard Chris moving in the bed. When she turned to go to the bathroom, he caught her in his arms and kissed her with such intensity it took her breath away.

He smiled at her, cherishing her with his eyes, and said softly, "Come back to bed with me. We can't get through to Wailuku, and I'd much rather spend the rest of the day making love to you."

She laughed huskily, considering the proposal, then asked, "And what about plan B?"

The light in his eyes dimmed, and he relaxed his hold on her. "I guess you're right. Mark will be looking for us. If we don't show up, the whole damn county police force will be searching for us, and they can't afford the expense." He paused and grinned at her. "But I'll take a rain check."

"You're on, Detective Sergeant Hadley."

"Instead of washing up here, why don't you come down to the bathhouse? We can bathe together."

"No thanks. I don't think I'm ready to go totally native just yet."
Chris picked up the kimono and wrapped it around himself. Claudia went into the bathroom that wasn't a complete bathroom. Its only fixtures were a washbasin and a toilet. It would have to do until she could get a shower someplace else.

Washed and dressed, with her hair dried and combed and wearing dry clothes, Claudia crossed the room to the veranda. She stood with the doors open, soaking up the peace and tranquility of this isolated piece of paradise and thinking of Chris.

Suddenly, Brutus started barking ferociously. Claudia stepped to the edge of the veranda and looked down the slope toward the shop building, where the road entered the yard. Two men were coming down the road on foot. They were wearing dark suits and walking very quietly. Instinctively, Claudia knew they didn't belong there. Brutus was raging at the end of his rope and threatening to break free. One of the men moved his arm to his coat and brought out a gun. As Claudia watched, the man pointed the gun at Brutus. She heard a muffled pop, and Brutus slumped to the ground and was quiet.

Claudia backed away from the railing and whirled into the bedroom. Chris had left his gun on the chest. Claudia pulled it from the holster. It was a nine-millimeter automatic, similar to the one she owned and had practiced with while taking her personal protection class. She released the clip in the butt and saw it was fully loaded. She snapped it back into place with the heel of her hand. She slid off the safety and ran to the door, her heart in her throat, knowing Chris was outside and unarmed.

She took a deep breath, pulled open the door, and yelled, "Chris! Look out!"

One man was standing close to the lower end of the bathhouse wall. He had spotted Jack and the boys beyond the building. The other man was walking toward the house and was almost to the point where he would be able to see Chris. Both men heard her, and their reactions were immediate. Claudia was already dropping into a crouching position on the porch of the guesthouse. As their guns came up from their sides and swung toward her, she was squeezing the trigger of the automatic. It exploded three times. The man nearest her went down, and the second man ducked behind the concrete-block wall at the end of the bathhouse.

Claudia saw a flash of white skin from the corner of her eye as she fired another round of three bullets into the wall where the second man had taken cover. Chris, totally naked, ran to the downed man and picked up the man's gun. He leaped back onto bathhouse deck, ran across the deck and around the end of the bathhouse, and disappeared.

Claudia turned her attention back to the block wall. From the corner of her eye, she saw movement to her right. It was Jack and his sons, running right into the middle of danger.

She yelled, "Jack, get down!" and pumped three more shots into the wall under the bathhouse.

Just then she saw movement at the end of the concrete wall and heard the pop of a gun. She was frozen with fear and waited long, heart-stopping moments. The hands holding Chris's gun were beginning to shake.

Two bare arms with guns dangling from the index finger of both hands appeared above the top of the wall. Claudia slowly lowered the pistol and rose to her feet, weak and trembling. Chris stepped out from behind the concrete wall and started walking across the grass toward her, totally naked and absolutely the second most gorgeous man she had ever seen in her life.

Claudia raced down the steps of the porch, the pistol heavy in her hand, and ran down the path toward Chris, needing to hold him and know he was safe and unharmed. He bent over to lay the guns down and straightened up to enclose her in his arms. She felt the trembling of his body as they held each other wordlessly.

CHAPTER XVI

"Why the bloody hell are two assassins coming here after you?"

Chris answered, "They weren't after me. They were after Claudia. She's in protective custody. I was trying to get her back to Wailuku."

Jack turned his gaze to Claudia. "Bloody good shot you are. You just saved Chris's bloody balls."

Claudia smiled weakly and said, "They're worth saving."

Jack erupted in laughter, and his sons grinned. Chris's tanned face darkened visibly.

"Well, what do you want to do with the bloody buggers?"

"Guess we'll have to haul them to Wailuku in the back of the truck."

"The bloody buggers shot Brutus."

"I'll get you a new dog, Jack. A bigger, meaner one."

Jack grinned at Chris and said, "Go get the truck, boys." Then he turned back to Chris and said, "I'd better go find Luke. She's probably under the bloody bed."

He turned away from them and headed at a run toward the house. Claudia started to laugh. Chris reached for the two guns on the grass, grabbed Claudia's hand, and pulled her after him toward the guesthouse, her laughter nearly hysterical.

He got her inside the guesthouse and took the gun out of her hand. She sat on the bed looking at him, and her laughter turned to tears and great, anguished sobs as the reality of what had just happened registered. She had actually killed someone with a gun. In her worst nightmares, she had not realized the full impact of actually taking a human life.

Chris got down on his knees in front of her and took her in his arms, holding her, his voice soothing as he said, "It's okay, Claudia. It's over. You're safe now. Shhh."

She finally stopped crying. Her hands went to his face, touching his cheeks, his mouth, and smoothing the lock of hair back from his forehead. Her voice trembled as she said, "I was so afraid for you."

"I was damn lucky to have you for a backup. Remind me never to be skeptical about women and guns again. Where the hell did you learn to shoot like that?"

"I told you I took a self-protection course."

"I know, but most women never follow up on it and practice what they are taught."

"Most women weren't raped before they took one of those courses. I practice at least once a month."

"Raped! My God, Claudia! How? When?"

"I was waiting for the bus in front of my office building. It was late and it was dark. My mind was somewhere else. A man hit me from behind and dragged me into the alley. I was left unconscious and found by the building maintenance man. I was tested for sexually transmitted diseases, and I lived in horror that I could be pregnant or become HIV-positive from that assault. I promised myself that would never happen to me again. I got a gun. I took the classes. I convinced my doctor to give me pregnancy protection." She covered her face with her hands.

"Oh, God, Claudia. I didn't realize. What can I say? Thank God you were here and knew how to handle a gun." He took her in his arms and held her for anxious moments. "Are you going to be okay?"

She took a deep breath. "Yes. You need to get some clothes on."

He grinned at her. "Yeah. Detective Hadley, the bare-assed crime fighter."

She smiled at that. "You did look funny walking around wearing nothing but a gun on each hand."

He stood, picked up the kimono she had worn, and put it on. This time he took his gun with him. "My clothes are down at the bathhouse. I'll be right back."

Claudia watched him all the way to the bathhouse. Jack came out of the house and yelled at him. "Lucky's got breakfast ready."

They ate breakfast and said their good-byes to Luke and the boys. Chris helped Claudia climb into the truck and got in beside her. Jack started the truck and shifted into low gear. They ground down the drive through banana palms, then uphill, toward the main road running through the little village of Kahakuloa. A canvas stretched over the back protected their cargo.

They turned onto the paved road. Jack shifted the truck into second gear, and almost immediately they were climbing up a steep grade on the cliff overlooking the village. The road was hardly wide enough for two cars to pass. The views from the truck window were spectacular, but Claudia only glanced at them briefly between the frequent blind corners winding around sheer, black cliffs. Her heart was in her throat most of the time, and she thought it was a good thing. Otherwise, she would be suffering from car sickness.

They had traveled in second and third gear for a half hour when they found the slide blocking the road around one of the blind curves. Jack was almost into it before he got the truck stopped.

"Well, this is it, mates. You're on your own from here."

Chris got out of the truck, and Claudia followed him. Chris went to the edge of the road and opened his cell phone. There was battery left, and he punched in some numbers and waited.

"Mark, it's CC. I'm on 340 about halfway to Wailuku. I need a meat wagon and a backhoe with a blade." He listened for a moment. "I'll tell you when you get here. My battery's about gone. Now it is gone."

Chris put the dead phone back in his belt holder. Jack was taking the canvas off the back of the truck.

"What you want done with these bloody bastards?"

"I'd like to feed them to the sharks, but I'd better keep them as evidence. Let's get them onto the canvas and into the shade. I'll let the meat wagon boys worry about how they're going to get them across the slide."

Claudia stayed on the ocean side of the truck while Jack and Chris unloaded the cargo and nestled the canvas-wrapped bodies against the cliff next to the slide. They came back to the driver's side of the truck when they were done, and Jack approached her.

"It was a pleasure meetin' you, Claudia. I wish you the best of luck with this bloody cop here. Take care."

Claudia put her arms around the man from Down Under and gave him a hug. "Thank you for everything, Jack. I hope we will meet again some day."

For once, Jack was speechless, his face a shade or two darker than normal. He tipped his hat, climbed back into the truck, started it, and put it in reverse. He would have to back the truck down the road until he found a wide spot to turn around in.

Claudia looked at Chris questioningly. "What do we do now?"

"We can wait here, or we can see if we can get across this slide and walk."

"I'd like to walk, if you don't mind." She eyed the canvas.

"Let me see if we can get across this."

Chris set his bag on the blacktop and climbed out into the mass of rocks, mud, and brush washed down from the cliffs above. Claudia watched him with apprehension as he inched his way forward, slipping and sliding in the unstable mass.

"Chris, come back!" She yelled. "It's too dangerous."

He turned. As he did, the mass shifted, and Chris's feet went out from under him. Claudia screamed as she saw him sliding toward the edge. He grabbed at a bush as he slipped over the edge of the cliff. He caught it and hung there precariously.

"Oh my God, Chris! Stay there. Don't move."

She could still hear the sound of Jack's truck grinding backwards down the road. Frantic, she ran after him, running like her life depended on it—only it was Chris's life depending on her.

Claudia rounded a curve and saw Jack backing up the grade on the other end of the curve. She waved and yelled frantically, trying to get his attention. A vehicle coming along the road behind Jack stopped him. Claudia pulled off her sweatshirt and waved it at him. He threw the truck into gear and came careening around the curve toward her.

He stopped long enough for her to get in. "Where's Chris?"

"He was trying to get across the slide. He's hanging on to a bush at the edge of the cliff."

Jack rammed the truck into gear again, and when the car behind him honked at him, he stuck his hand out the window in a one-fingered salute and yelled, "Stick it in your ear, you bloody bastard!"

Claudia was almost afraid to look when they reached the slide—afraid Chris wouldn't be there. She closed her eyes against what she might see, but she couldn't keep from looking. She had to know! She saw his arms, still wrapped around the bush. It was canted over the edge as Chris's weight slowly uprooted it.

Jack set the emergency brake on the truck, leaving it running. Before he bailed out of the seat he said, "I'm going to need your help."

"What can I do?"

"Meet me around front."

Then he was out the door. Claudia opened her door and got down from the truck.

Someone in the car behind them yelled, "What's going on, lady?"

She yelled back, "This slide blocks the whole road. You can't get through. Go back the way you came."

Jack was already in front of the truck. He had the rope that had held the canvas over the truck bed and was tying it to the heavy steel bumper. As he wrapped the other end of the rope around his waist, he told her, "I'm going to take the winch cable out to him. I need you to operate the winch." His eyes squinted questioningly at her as he finished knotting the rope around himself. "Do you think you can do it?"

Claudia swallowed hard and answered more confidently than she felt. "Show me what I need to do."

Jack bent over the winch and flipped a lever on it. "When you see he's got a good grip on the cable, you pull this lever back and push this button here." His finger lightly touched a red button.

Before she could even nod that she understood, Jack was headed for the slide, reeling the steel cable off as he went. Jack was almost to Chris. He reeled off more of the cable, coiled it, and threw it over the edge of the cliff. It landed in the bush, out of Chris's reach. Jack rolled the cable up, pulled a few more feet into the coil, and heaved it again.

This time, the cable uncoiled over the top of the bush. Chris grabbed it with one hand.

Jack yelled, "He's got it."

Claudia reached for the lever, pulled it forward, and hit the button. The winch groaned and uncoiled more cable. Claudia screamed in horror, afraid she had done something wrong. Then she heard the winch start to work. She watched as it pulled Chris slowly up until he was above the edge of the road and Jack could grab him by the arms. Claudia felt weak in the knees. She closed her eyes, whispering words of thanks that he was all right.

Jack was giving Chris a piece of his mind as they came down off the slide.

"You going to do anything else bloody stupid today, Detective Hadley, or can I leave you until the coppers get here?"

Claudia opened her eyes. Chris was mud from his chin to his shoes and looked duly chastised.

"Okay, okay! It was a stupid thing to do. I think you can leave me with Claudia."

Jack's mouth twisted in a grin. "That's twice today she's saved your bloody ass. I think it's you who needs protective custody." Then he turned a sly grin on Claudia and added, "I never seen his brain so addled. You better marry the poor bastard and put him out of his bloody misery."

Claudia said, "Thanks for the advice, Jack. And thanks for coming to our rescue again."

"Well, don't I rate another hug?"

Claudia willingly gave the Aussie a hug, and this time she kissed his cheek, too.

Jack blushed again and bent to shut off the winch. Jack looked up at Chris and asked, "You have asked her to marry you, haven't you?"

Chris, in the process of coiling up the rope, answered, "Yeah." He turned and walked to the back of the truck with the rope, leaving an awkward silence.

Jack looked at Claudia questioningly, "What'd you say?"

Claudia smiled and answered, "I haven't said yes."

Jack's mouth formed a silent "Oh." He climbed into his truck, released the brake, and put the truck in reverse to start backing down the road once more. Claudia waved at him.

Jack was gone around the corner when Chris said, "Listen. I think the troops have arrived on the other side."

Claudia listened. She was able to distinguish men's voices and a different set of engine noises. Relief flooded through her like a tidal wave. It had been little more than twenty-four hours since she and Chris had left the Lahaina Gardens Hotel, and she felt she had lived a lifetime. She reached for Chris's hand and held it tightly in hers. She looked up into his mud-smeared face and smiled.

It was an hour before the backhoe was able to clear a path through the slide. A short, wiry man with straight, black hair followed the backhoe through the cut. He had Oriental eyes, high cheekbones, and a square jaw. He stopped when he saw Chris, his dark, almond-shaped eyes widening in disbelief. Then an amused grin split his face. The laugh lines at the corners of his youthful face deepened as his eyes squinted almost shut with humor. He had a boyish, mischievous smile. He was shorter than Chris by at least a half a foot. He was even shorter than Claudia, but what she saw of him looked promising if she ever pursued Chris's idea of using male models. Behind him came a cadre of policemen. Chris released her hand.

Trying to control his amusement, the man Claudia assumed was Mark asked, "What in Buddha's name happened to you?"

"It's a long story. I'll tell you about it later. I've got a couple of dead men over here. By the way, this is Claudia Jordan. Claudia, this is Detective Mark Mitsuro."

Claudia looked at Chris. She sensed a change in him, and she wondered what was going on. He didn't seem happy to see Mark. She could sense a reserve in him that hadn't been there before, and then she realized he was officially back on the job.

Mark looked up at her and smiled, offering her his hand. "You're everything Chris said you were. It's nice to finally get to meet you."

Claudia took his hand. His hand held hers in a firm grip, and he did a respectful Oriental bow. The eyes he raised to hers were friendly and honest.

"Thank you. Chris has told me a lot about you, too."

Chris bent to pick up their bags and said, "I'm going to take Claudia to the car and change into some clean clothes. Do a check on those dead men, and then let's get out of here. I'll give you a blow-by-blow account once we're on the road."

"Roger."

Mark went to join the group of policemen already looking at the bodies under the canvas. Claudia turned away and followed Chris to the other side of the slide. He opened the door of an unmarked police car, and Claudia got in.

"I'll be back in a minute. I'm going to change in the lab truck."

Claudia leaned her head against the seat of the car. She closed her eyes against the tumult of emotions filling her now that she and Chris were safe.

The car door opened, and Claudia sat up with a start. It was Mark. He slid into the seat behind the wheel of the car and said, "Sorry I startled you. How'd you get here with two dead bodies and no sailboat?" He grinned at her, and she knew he was trying to put her at ease.

"Do you know Jack Cain? From Kahakuloa?"

"Yeah, I know the bloody Aussie. You put in there last night?"

"Yes."

Chris returned to the car and got in the front seat with Mark.

"Can you get us out of here?"

Mark said, "I can try."

He pulled forward, then put the car in reverse and started backing down the road past the other police cars and the large, vanlike vehicle that would haul the dead men back to Wailuku.

As the car wove back and forth, Chris warned, "Claudia gets seasick."

"We're not on a boat."

"I don't think her stomach can tell the difference."

There was a turnout on the edge of the cliff. Mark backed into it and turned the car around. Then, at a much slower and gentler speed, he headed down the road. "Now, will you tell me what the hell happened?"

"We beached the sailboat at Kahakuloa Bay yesterday just before dark and spent the night with Aussie Jack. This morning I left Claudia in the guesthouse and went over to Jack's bathhouse. I was in the tub when Jack's dog started raising hell. I heard a pop and found a knothole in the wall around the tub to look through. There were these two hit men walking toward me, headed for Jack's house. Claudia came out of the guesthouse with my gun and yelled at me. She dropped into a crouch and fired. I could see through the knothole that one was down. Claudia was firing shots at the other one, who had taken cover around the corner of the bathhouse. I came out of the tub and grabbed the gun off the one Claudia put down. While she covered me, I went around the back side of the bathhouse and nailed the second one."

"And that's all there was to it?"

"Yeah."

"Now let me get this straight. You're taking a bath, which I presume means you were naked and unarmed?"

Chris gave Mark a dark glance. "I didn't say that."

"And Claudia shot the first gunner and kept the other one at bay while you grabbed the first gunner's piece and ran around the bathhouse, naked as a jaybird, and shot the second gunner? Do I have facts correct, Detective Sergeant Hadley?"

Mark's face in the rearview mirror was contorted with his effort to keep from laughing. Claudia, remembering the scene as Mark described it, started to giggle.

Chris gave them both dark looks, and Mark burst out laughing.

"I can't wait until you file this report, bruddah!"

"It wasn't funny."

Between spasms of laughter, Mark asked, "Then why is Claudia laughing?"

Chris retorted, annoyed, "She's hysterical."

"Saved your butt is more like it, bruddah."

Chris frowned, and Claudia controlled her laughter.

Now she understood. His ego was suffering. He had made all the wrong choices, and if it hadn't been for Claudia, he would have been dead—not once, but twice. If he filed a report stating the events as they had really happened at Kahakuloa, he would lose all credibility with the police department. And now Claudia felt guilty, too. She knew what happened between her and Chris had not helped him perform his job. He was in love with her, and that had outweighed everything else. She could understand it, but could his superiors?

Mark, seeming to become aware of Chris's discomfort at his shrewd analysis of the situation, made an effort to control his laughter and drove for several miles with apparent concentration on the road, which was gradually becoming better as they neared Wailuku.

Finally, Mark asked, "Do you want to tell me the rest of it?"

"No. It wasn't in the line of duty."

Claudia heard the anger in Chris's answer. Mark said, "I'm sorry, Chris. I didn't mean to shoot you down like that. What do you want me to do?"

Chris's voice was less defensive when he answered, "There's nothing you can do. I screwed up, and I'll have to take the heat."

Mark asked, "Claudia, didn't he do everything in his power to protect you?"

"Yes. Everything he did, he did for me. He left his gun with me because I couldn't go to the bathhouse with him, could I?"

"*Ahso.* Good point, Claudia. And you just happen to be Annie Oakley, right?"

Chris interrupted, "Come on, Mark! Let it alone."

Claudia said, "No, Chris. This is important. Mark doesn't know this, but yes, I can shoot a gun. I'm certified by the state of New York to carry a concealed weapon. I've taken advanced personal protection classes, and I practice gun handling on a regular basis."

Mark beamed. "Wow! Right on!"

"No, it's not!" Chris said. "You can whitewash this all you want, but the fact is, I lost my objectivity in this thing, and there is no way either one of you can change that."

Mark glanced at Claudia in the rearview mirror and shrugged. Claudia shook her head. Everything else would have to be left unsaid.

CHAPTER XVII

They pulled into the parking area in front of the police station and got out of the car. As they climbed the steps to the left of the main entrance, Chris took her arm and went through the door with her. Claudia saw the red lights flashing inside the juvenile office to the right, and it reminded her she still had her derringer in her pocket. If they discovered it, she and Chris could be in more hot water.

The Hawaiian at the desk inside the office window smiled at them and said, "How's it going, Sergeant Hadley?"

Chris forced a smile and answered, "You don't want to know."

Claudia glanced at Mark, and he made a wry face. The desk officer looked puzzled but didn't ask any more questions. They went down the corridor to the office where they had questioned Claudia before, and Chris ushered her through the door.

Chris started giving Mark instructions, "Call Lahaina PD and have them pick up Miss Jordan's luggage at the Hotel. Call Henri and let him know they're coming for it, and have it delivered here."

He stopped at the end of the first partition and said, "Pake, I want you to find out what Miss Jordan would like for lunch and go get it for her."

Claudia said, "Anything will be fine."

Pake rolled her chair to the end of the partition and called, "A hamburger?"

"Yes, that's fine."

The pressure from Chris's hand on her elbow signaled he was ready to move on. He opened the door to the interrogation room.

"There will be a couple of detectives in to take a statement from you. As soon as Mark is free, I'll have him see about getting you on a flight back to the mainland. Hopefully, this will all be taken care of in a couple of hours."

He turned, walked out the door, and left her and Mark staring at each other. Claudia sank onto the hard chair in despair.

Even Mark looked confused. He said into the awkward silence, "Anything I can get for you?"

She shook her head. "No, thank you. I'm all right."

But she was far from all right. The man who had brought her into the station was not the same man who had made love to her last night and this morning. She could understand why. What she couldn't understand was why he was not communicating with her. And why was he sending her away? How could she testify about this morning and the car she saw the day she went with David to meet Puna on the back side of Haleakala?

The door opened, and Detective Cave and Detective Omoto entered the room. Detective Cave said, "Hello again, Miss Jordan. We need to get a statement from you. Will you cooperate with us?"

"I'll try."

"That's fair. We'll be taping this just like we did before. Will you agree to that?"

"Yes."

They pulled out the chairs across the table from her and sat down. Detective Omoto set down the tape machine, plugged it into the outlet next to the table, turned it on, and said, "You may begin now, Miss Jordan. Please state your full name and place of residence."

"My name is Claudia Jane Jordan, and my state of residence is New York."

Detective Cave asked, "Please tell us in your own words what happened this morning at the Jack Cain residence at Kahakuloa, and why you were there."

"As you know, I was in the protective custody of Detective Hadley. He decided it was no longer safe to keep me in Lahaina and believed the safest way to transport me to Wailuku was on his boat. We put into the bay at Kahakuloa yesterday, just before dark.

"We were staying in Jack Cain's guesthouse. There were no bathing facilities in the guesthouse. Detective Hadley left to use Mr. Cain's bathhouse so I could wash and dress in privacy."

"And why did Detective Hadley leave his weapon with you?"

"I suppose he didn't feel he needed it."

"Then you didn't think it unusual for Detective Hadley to leave you and leave his gun with you?"

"No. He had no reason to believe anyone knew where we were. He had no reason to believe that he would need his gun."

"Can you explain why Detective Hadley would leave you to go take a bath?"

"I told you. The guesthouse had no bathing facilities."

"What was your reason for not wanting to use the bathhouse?"

Claudia felt a flush of warmth begin deep within her. She tried to keep it from reaching her face. "Mr. Cain's tub is not indoors and it is not a bathtub, but more like a hot tub. I preferred to stay in the guesthouse. Detective Hadley has done everything he could to protect me and be sensitive to my privacy during this ordeal."

The detectives exchanged glances with raised eyebrows. Detective Cave continued, "What happened while Detective Hadley was at the bathhouse?"

"Mr. Cain's dog started to bark. I went out onto the veranda to see what was causing the disturbance. The dog was tied to a palm tree in the yard. I saw two men walking into the yard, and one of the men shot the dog."

"Why did you look to see what the dog was barking at? Is it because you were expecting someone?"

Claudia frowned at the question. "Absolutely not. I looked because the dog sounded furious."

"You know when a dog sounds furious? Come, now. This is a dog you had just seen for the first time, right?"

"I resent your implication, Detective Cave. My family always had a dog when I was growing up. You can tell the difference between a dog barking at a squirrel running up a tree from a bark when he feels threatened."

Again, a glance and nod between the two men questioning her. "Please continue, Miss Jordan."

"I knew Detective Hadley had no way of protecting himself, since he had left his gun with me. I took the gun to the front door of the guesthouse and yelled a warning to Detective Hadley. Both men had guns and they would have shot me, but I was able to shoot one of them first. The other man ran behind a wall at the end of the bathhouse. Detective Hadley used the dead man's gun and shot the other gunman without harm to anyone else."

"You are telling us you used Detective Hadley's weapon to kill one of the men?"

"Yes."

"How were you able to do that, Miss Jordan?"

"Detective Hadley knew I had taken personal protection instruction and that I have a permit to carry a gun in the state of New York."

"And how did he know that, Miss Jordan?"

Claudia's mind raced for wording that wouldn't reveal she had a gun on her person. "I mentioned it to Detective Hadley."

"Why would you just mention it to someone?"

"He wanted to know, if something should happen to him, if I would be able to use a gun in my defense."

"And you knew how to use the particular weapon that he carries?"

"Yes. I practice on a regular basis with a similar gun."

The detectives exchanged glances, and Detective Omoto asked, "What is your reason for needing a weapon for your personal protection, Miss Jordan?"

Claudia hesitated. "I don't see what that has to do with this."

Detective Cave answered, "It has everything to do with this. You were seeing a man we suspect of drug dealing. How do we know you are not involved in that felony? Someone is out to kill everyone who was in on this particular deal. You are definitely involved, Miss Jordan. Now, let me repeat the question. What is your reason for wanting to be able to shoot someone?"

Reluctantly, she answered, "I had a bad experience. I do not wish to repeat it."

"How bad?"

She bit her lip. They were not going to be satisfied until they knew every detail of her life. In a harsh voice, she answered, "I was standing in front of my office building waiting for my bus. It was dark, it was raining, and I was preoccupied. A man grabbed me and dragged me into an alley. I was raped and robbed. That is when I decided I was going to be prepared for the next time."

There were no glances between the men, just a lowering of eyes as Claudia finished her statement.

Just then, Pake came in with a sack and set it on the table for her. The aroma of hamburger and fries filled the room. Claudia's stomach responded with a growl.

Detective Omoto shut off the tape machine. "Thank you, Miss Jordan."

The detectives rose and left the room. Claudia went limp. She had been more stressed than she realized. She said a silent prayer that she had said nothing that might jeopardize Chris. Because of his love for her, he had put his life and his job on the line to keep her safe.

Claudia finished her hamburger and waited, her tension returning as the minutes passed. When Chris finally came into the room, she almost knocked the chair over getting to her feet. She had expected him to take her in his arms and tell her everything was all right, but he didn't.

"Okay, Miss Jordan. Detective Mitsuro has gotten a flight time for you for tomorrow afternoon out of Honolulu. Your luggage is on its way from Lahaina. As soon as it arrives, Detective Mitsuro will take you to Honolulu and stay with you until your plane leaves."

Claudia choked back the sob filling her throat. "Thank you."

He nodded and left the room. She wanted to run after him but stood rooted to the floor, unable to move. She was still standing there, wounded and stunned by what was happening, when Mark came into the room.

"Your luggage just arrived from Lahaina. I can take you to the airport now."

Chris came back into the room and closed the door. "I forgot to tell you, Mark. Don't let anyone search her. She's got a gun in her pocket."

Mark paled. "You've got to be kidding!"

Chris gave him a crooked smile and shook his head. He barely glanced at Claudia before he turned to leave the room again.

Mark looked at her and asked, "Are you ready to go?"

On the verge of tears, she stuttered, "Yes."

They left the building, Mark holding on to her elbow until he handed her into his car. A uniformed officer followed them, and Mark opened the trunk of the car for her luggage. Soon he climbed in beside her.

Claudia held her silence until they were on Kaahumanu Avenue heading for the airport. Then she said, "Will you please tell me what is going on?"

He glanced at her and grinned. "Well, Chris has got himself in one very tight sling. I think your statement helped, but he's going to be sitting at a desk for the rest of the week, filling out paperwork. The good news is he got you out of here because of your part in fingering Phnom and the action you took to save his life. But that doesn't get him off the hook. He knows he bent the rules, and now he's got to pay the price."

"But the way he acted. He was a different man than the one ..." She stopped, flushing at the memories, and finished lamely, "I'm used to."

Mark glanced at her with a knowing smile. "He lost his objectivity when he fell in love with you, and he knows it. He's got to get his head on straight, or he's done for. He loves you, and when he's through this, he'll get in touch with you. I'll do everything I can to help him."

The tears coursed down Claudia's cheeks. Mark saw them and reached out to take her hand.

"Don't worry, Claudia. He's a fine cop and a fine man. He's got to get his act together before he can face you. And you can be sure he will."

They got to the airport and parked the car. Claudia remembered her derringer and said, "I need to put this gun in my luggage before we go in."

They opened the trunk, and Claudia opened her suitcase. She removed the bullets from her gun, locked it in its steel case, and put the bullets in her second bag.

Mark whistled. "How did Chris find out about the gun?"

She smiled and answered, "That's how I met him. It set off the hotel security system he installed."

"I'll be damned! And he let you keep it?"

"No. It was in the hotel safe all the time I was there. He had me take it with me when we got on the boat."

"Geez! I hope no one knows this but me."

"No one does."

"Well, let's get going before the tourists get all the seats."

The flight to Honolulu was short. Claudia was quiet, unable to forget the thoughts of Chris and their night together in their own private paradise. She wondered if she would ever find that paradise again.

Mark called for a cab, and they were soon being transported to a hotel near the airport, where they would spend the night. Claudia was finally able to suppress her feelings and thoughts. She talked with Mark about her work, his family, and all the unimportant things people talk about when they are trying to avoid what they really want to talk about. Claudia wanted to talk about Chris.

Mark slept on the twin bed next to her, but Claudia couldn't sleep and was glad to finally get up and get away. Everything here reminded her of what she had lost and what she was still losing. It was time for her to go home to New York, where she could concentrate on her work instead of memories.

They had breakfast in the hotel, and then took the hotel shuttle to the Honolulu airport. They got her luggage checked through, and Mark took her to the gate. He sat with her while they were waiting for her plane to load and escorted her to the plane door when she could finally board.

She turned before stepping through into the plane and said, "Thanks, Mark. I appreciate all you've done for me. I'm glad Chris has you for a friend."

He gave her a smile and reached for her hand, saying, "It was my pleasure, Miss Jordan. Have a good flight."

Claudia ignored his hand and gave him a hug. The top of his head came to her chin, and when she released him, his cheeks were darkened and his grin showed his embarrassment. He backed away from her and she turned, stepping through the doorway into the plane. Her seat in first class was on the opposite side of the plane from the door. She settled into it, tired now, and closed her eyes.

◆　　◆　　◆

To say that Phnom Latmeong was upset would be an understatement. The threat to his livelihood, even his very life, had begun when David Keanu brought his lady friend along to a drug deal that was to have been between David, Puna, and Puna's two brothers. There was no doubt in Phnom's mind that Claudia Jordan had put the finger on him by giving the police his license number. Not to mention that David and Puna had made another stupid move when they gave Claudia a locked suitcase with drugs in it to take to Los Angeles. Someone had to pay for those mistakes, and Phnom was making sure it wasn't going to be him. He was getting rid of the people involved. It was amazing how much information he could obtain from people in inconspicuous jobs like a janitor at the airport, or a busboy at a hotel, for money or drugs. Unfortunately, his hired assassins had been unable to take care of the one person who could still possibly identify him. Fortunately, Phnom had favors he could call in, and he was able to find out that Claudia Jordan was about to fly out of Honolulu. He learned Claudia's flight number and seat number. He reserved the first-class seat next to her. He had even devised a plan to get her off the plane and eliminate the threat she posed to him. As the plane was loading, he called in a bomb threat from a pay phone in the airport before he boarded the plane. All he had to do was let fate take its course.

◆ ◆ ◆

Someone stopped in the aisle next to Claudia's seat. She was aware of a bag being stuffed under the seat and someone settling into the seat beside her. There was the brush of a hand against her as the person groped for and fastened the seat belt. Claudia shifted in her seat, turning closer to the window, and kept her eyes closed. The flight attendants were in the aisles, closing the overhead compartments and checking seatbelts. She heard the plane doors close and felt the air pressure change as the engines were turned on, cooling the muggy warmth of the cabin. She felt the plane start moving backwards, away from the terminal. Then, just as Claudia was drifting into sleep, everything shut down. The cool air turned warm again. Claudia opened her eyes in the half-light of a powerless plane. Her breath caught in her throat as she wondered at the unusual delay.

The captain's voice broke into the buzz of speculation around her. "May I have your attention, please? Ladies and gentlemen, this is Captain Hara. Please remain in your seats and keep your seat belts fastened. There will be a short delay. Power will be back on in a minute or two."

Claudia sighed. She closed her eyes against the delay and the rapidly warming, humid air, wanting only to sleep. She felt the plane move as they were towed back to the gate. Soon she felt the air move again through the plane and knew power had been restored.

CHAPTER XVIII

Chris was sitting at a desk, working on his report. He had to remember every detail of the last twenty-four hours, and the harder he tried, the more frustrated he got. He couldn't keep his mind from miring in the memory of Claudia and how she had looked at him, not understanding why he was sending her away. And now he didn't understand why he had let her go, either. All he could think of was that she was alone and vulnerable. He should have gone with her, even if it meant his job. He realized now that the job didn't matter. All that mattered was Claudia, and she was gone.

The police radio caught his attention. He turned up the volume as the message was repeated. A cold chill ran over him as he heard the voice say, "An anonymous caller has just reported a bomb on board United flight 172 for Los Angeles. All available units are to report to the Honolulu airport."

Chris came out of his chair, knocking it over as he ran to the front desk. Pake looked up from her work, startled.

"Where's the helicopter? I've got to get to Honolulu."

"No helicopter. Besides, you're grounded. Remember?"

"Not anymore. There's a bomb report on Miss Jordan's flight. *Now where's the helicopter?*"

"It's in for repair."

"It's been in for repair for months!"

Pake shrugged. "No funds. No repair."

"Then call for a charter, and get them here fast!"

"But you don't have authorization to do that."

He grimaced in frustration, seeing Claudia dying in his mind. "I don't give a damn! *Now get me a chopper!*"

He turned on his heel and raced back to his desk. He had to reach Mark. He called Mark's cell phone and got his voice mail. Groaning, he got the dial tone again, called Mark's pager, and hoped. His gun lay on his desk. He picked it up, checked it, refilled the cartridge, and rammed it home. He holstered the weapon and buckled on the harness. His phone rang as he put on his jacket.

"Mark?"

"Yeah. What's up?"

"I just heard Claudia's flight has had a bomb threat. I'm getting a chopper and coming over. Get to that gate as fast as you can."

He heard the concern in Mark's voice as he said, "Shit! You think it's Phnom?"

"I'd bet on it. Be careful."

"I'm on my way."

The phone went dead. Chris cradled his receiver, dug into the bag he'd brought from Lahaina, found the box of shells he'd packed, and headed back to the front desk.

Pake said, "A chopper is on the way."

Chris gave her a smile of appreciation and said, "Thanks, Pake. I owe you one." He headed for the door.

Outside, he heard the helicopter coming and looked up. He waved at it with both arms, and it settled down in the parking lot. Chris ran for the door with his back bent. The copter's blades created a whirlwind of dust that tore at his clothes and stung his eyes. He opened the door and climbed in.

The pilot had a graying ponytail pulled through the back of his baseball cap. He wore dark, wraparound glasses, cutoffs, and an oil-stained T-shirt with the logo "Defecation Happens." "Where to, Pal?"

Chris settled himself in the seat and fastened the seatbelt as the chopper lifted off the ground. "Honolulu airport. I have a witness on United flight 172 to LA that has just had a bomb threat. How fast can this thing go?"

The thin, pockmarked face of the pilot turned to him with a grin. "We're about to find out."

Chris looked at him with wide eyes, afraid to ask his next question but too concerned about self-preservation not to. "What does that mean?"

His pilot grinned and answered, "It means this is a brand-new bird. She hasn't been completely put through her paces, so we're going to find out together. By the way, I'm Skip. You got a name? I gotta get clearance to land at Lulu."

"Detective Sergeant Hadley of Maui County PD. Claudia Jordan is my witness on that United flight."

Skip hung a headset over the top of his baseball cap and said, "Get me Honolulu airport. I need clearance."

Chris listened as the pilot explained the situation and finally signed off with, "Roger."

"Does that mean we're in?"

"Yup. We can land on the top of the parking garage. The Lulu police are setting up a command post there."

"That's not close enough."

Skip chuckled. "Well, I could get you closer, but there'd be hell to pay. Besides, I like my job."

Chris looked out the window. They had already crossed the Maui isthmus and were skimming over the water so quickly his eyes blurred. He looked out the front window and saw Lanai looming ahead. He looked at his watch. Maybe he would be in time.

◆ ◆ ◆

Inside the grounded airplane, long minutes passed. The passengers were getting restless, and the flight attendants were losing credibility in their efforts to convince everyone the delay would last only a little longer. Claudia was wide-awake now and getting more concerned with each passing minute. The humidity in the airplane was winning the battle over the inadequate air system, and her patience was getting as thin as everyone else's.

Finally, the speaker system came on and the captain's voice brought quiet. "This is your captain speaking. I'm very sorry for the delay. I know you are uncomfortable, and I thank you for your patience. However, due to circumstances beyond our control, we are going to start deplaning at this time. Please remain seated until the flight attendants get to you. Please do not take any luggage off the plane and do not block the aisle. Women may take their purses, but all other bags must remain on board. Thank you for your cooperation."

Claudia started to reach under the seat for her purse. Her seatmate's hand stopped her. She turned questioning eyes on the man she had hardly noticed before. She felt a cold chill envelop her flushed skin as she looked into the face of a slight, dark-haired man with Asian features.

"Please do not move until I tell you to. I have a syringe in my pocket with enough drugs to kill you if you do not obey me."

Claudia settled back in her seat, numb with fear. She had no gun—nothing to protect herself from this man who had killed David, Puna, and Puna's brothers. And now he was going to kill her, unless ...

◆   ◆   ◆

In the speeding chopper, Chris checked and rechecked his watch every few seconds. Diamond Head loomed straight ahead of him. He was to the point of hyperventilating. He was telling himself for the hundredth time to stay calm and breathe.

The chopper pilot enthusiastically yelped, "Hot dog!" They zipped up and over the top of Diamond Head like an express elevator, leaving Chris's stomach on the beach. "Wish I'd had this baby in Nam. She's a mover! Good maneuverability, too. I could land this baby right on top of that United plane."

Chris dared to ask, "You've never flown this bird before?"

"Well, not exactly. We've been doin' all the ground checks on her. That's my job. I'm the guy who makes sure they're gonna get off the ground. But not to worry, Sarge. I flew choppers in Nam until I got shot out of the sky. Kinda lost my desire to fly after that, so I pretty much stay on the ground. But man, I'm kinda enjoyin' this."

Chris didn't ask any more questions. He could see the Honolulu airport ahead. Skip was on the radio again, getting clearance to land the chopper. They went down with all the speed of a roller coaster and softly landed.

When Chris's stomach caught up and he could breathe again, he held out his hand to Skip and said, "You're one hell of a pilot. Thanks, Skip."

Skip grinned, shook his hand, and said, "No problem. Hope you make it."

"So do I," Chris yelled over his shoulder as he jumped down. Bent over, he ran toward the cluster of policemen a few yards away.

"Detective Sergeant Hadley of Maui County. I've got a witness on United 172. What's the situation?"

A stocky Hawaiian in plain clothes, his dark forehead glistening with sweat, answered, "They've just issued orders to get the passengers off the plane. You got any handle on what's goin' on?"

"I do, but I don't have time to give you all the details. I think the bomb threat is a hoax. They're after my witness. I'm going in. Don't follow me with uniforms, or my witness is dead."

"Okay, Hadley. We'll follow you in. Five men with plain clothes. Who we lookin' for?"

"An Asian drug dealer. Phnom Latmeong. He's on your list. He's put four down that we know of." His face contorted as an image of Claudia crossed his mind's eye. "I'm going in."

He sprinted across the parking lot toward the bridge to the terminal. He wasn't in the habit of praying, but he prayed now that he would be in time.

◆   ◆   ◆

The flight attendant stopped beside the seat where Claudia and her captor sat. His hand gripped her elbow painfully. They rose together and stepped out into the aisle with his hand on her elbow, guiding her in front of him. She walked nervously forward, looking for some way to escape, but there was no way to break away from him. They were behind other passengers, and there was nowhere to go.

When they were finally out of the plane, her captor repositioned himself at her side. His right hand still gripped her arm just above her elbow; his left hand was positioned above her elbow from the front, so it looked like she was supporting him. They followed the passengers through the Jetway and into the passenger holding area.

Claudia hesitated once they were out of the Jetway, but her captor propelled her forward with increased pressure on her elbow. She moved on, letting him guide her out into the concourse and toward the main terminal. Out of the main crush of deplaning passengers, her captor no longer kept his left hand on her arm; he kept it over the breast pocket of his suit, where the inside pocket held the syringe. They left the gate area and were walking through the long, open-air section of the concourse leading into the terminal. In the bright sunlight, Claudia could see the point of the needle through the ivory linen material of the man's suit jacket. She began to lose hope.

As the concourse merged with the main terminal, Claudia saw Mark standing just inside the security checkpoint. He saw her, and his face lit in a relieved smile. Claudia knew a moment of relief, too, before she realized Mark could trigger her death if he challenged her captor as a policeman. Her eyes pleaded with him to be careful.

Mark came up to her with a grin, saying, "Claudia, what a surprise. It's a small world, isn't it?. How have you been?"

Claudia slowed to a stop. Her captor gripped her arm so tightly she winced in pain, but she stood her ground. Her captor continued to apply a bruising, painful grip on her arm to keep her moving forward.

She smiled, "Mark. How good to see you." She extended her hand to him, and he took it, holding it securely, reassuringly. She continued, "I'd like you to meet a friend I met on the plane."

Mark released her hand and swung toward the slight Asian, his hand extended. The man's hand slipped inside the coat, and Claudia screamed, "Mark!"

Mark grabbed the man's wrist, yanking it away from the inside pocket. He grabbed the man's fingers with his other hand and bent them back until the man grimaced. Claudia felt the grip on her elbow loosen, and she tore her arm out of his grasp and yelled, "*Security! Help!*"

Mark released his grip on Phnom's fingers to reach for his handcuffs, stating, "I'm placing you under arrest."

Phnom, trapped, desperate, and skilled in martial arts, delivered a swift, hard, right-hand chop to Mark's neck.

Mark staggered backward, dazed. Phnom, seizing the advantage, used all his weight and brought his knee up hard into Mark's groin. Mark, already dazed, dropped his grip on Phnom and bent over, clutching his groin. Phnom knocked him down to the floor with another chop to the ear as the security guards rushed at him.

Claudia yelled, "Stop him! Don't let him get away!"

Phnom whirled out of reach and elbowed unsuspecting people out of his way as he escaped the security team. He ran through the detection gate, knocking down a woman ready to pass through.

Claudia went down on her knees beside Mark.

"Mark, are you all right?"

"Give me a minute. How about you?"

She gave him a wan smile. "I'm fine. Thank God you were here. How did you know?"

"Chris called me."

"Chris?" she questioned, the terror she had felt beginning to subside.

"Yeah. He heard the bomb report on the police radio."
"Is he here?" She dared to hope.
"I'd bet on it."
"Can you get up?"

Mark nodded. Claudia stood up expectantly and offered Mark her hand. He got to his feet a little tentatively, pain fleeting through his eyes as he tried to straighten up.

◆ ◆ ◆

Chris didn't want to trust the elevator. He leaped down the stairs two at a time, emerging in the American Airlines lobby area. The United lobby was the last one at the end of the building. The United flights used the gates on the Diamond Head Concourse, which curved eastward, away from the end of the building. To the left, separating the American lobby from the United lobby, a fruit, flower, and gift concession stood in the middle of the intersection leading to the gates. He charged forward, dodging people like a football player running through a field of tacklers. He didn't slow down until he could see the security check station stretching across the full width of the hall leading to the concourse.

He saw Claudia on the other side of the check station just as she yelled, "Stop him! Don't let him get away!"

He looked for Phnom, his heart racing. He focused his attention on the people at the check station. Then he saw a man break through the detection gate, knocking a woman down. He was running, dodging, and pushing people out of his way. Chris kept his eyes on the man, shutting Claudia out of his mind. The slight, black-haired man running toward him was all that mattered. He had to stop the man, no matter what the cost.

It took Phnom only seconds to cover the short distance between the security checkpoint and Chris. He dodged around Chris, who wheeled and launched himself at Phnom, tackling him from behind, hitting him in the middle of the back like a battering ram. The man went down hard, grunting in surprise. Chris pinned him down, grabbed an arm, and wrenched it up hard across the man's back in a hammerlock. The man was struggling and yelling hysterically in his native tongue, trying to free the arm Chris held. Chris yanked all the harder on the arm, and the man let out a cry and a groan, his body jerking in a convulsion.

Breathless himself from his run, Chris gasped, "You're under arrest. You have the right to remain silent. You have the right to council. You have …" He felt the man under him go limp and felt the very life seep out of his captive. Chris stood up and turned the man over just as Mark and a cadre of security reached him from behind and the police in plain clothes arrived from the front.

The man's coat was open on one side. The other side was pinned to his arm by a slender needle. Chris turned away, his face turning white. It could have been Claudia on the end of that needle.

Mark grabbed him, but he tore away. He saw Claudia, surrounded by airport security, and he went to her. She stepped out of the protective circle of guards and into his arms, shaking and crying, his name a sob on her lips.

"Oh, Chris. Thank God. I was so scared."

He held her, his eyes filled with tears and his voice shaking with relief as he whispered, "It's okay, sweetheart. It's over. I've got you now, and I'm never going to let you go."

THE END

978-0-595-45141-8
0-595-45141-1